Sunflower Kisses

Seeds of Love
Book 1

2nd Edition

J.B. Wittkofsky

Contents

I owe the courage, the will, and the guts to write this book to my wife. Gracie, you have always pushed me to be better, to be more than I ever thought was possible. You inspired me to pick up writing again and helped me rekindle my love for it. When I decided to write a romance book, it was your words that pushed me forward. Your faith in me, made me believe in myself. I dedicate this entire book to you, my love. You will always be my number one. Always and forever.

Clay, Meet Bailey

Twenty-one is an odd age. Yeah, you have the excitement of being able to legally drink, but I've been drinking for years. The allure just isn't there anymore. It's almost as if you're officially an adult. You look forward to turning sixteen to get your driver's license; you look forward to turning eighteen so you can gamble, and you look forward to turning twenty-one so you can legally drink and buy tobacco. What comes next? What do I look forward to next? My car insurance going down?

My life has been interesting to say the least. Coming from a homeless childhood while having several mental illnesses, I've pushed through just about everything. I just graduated college with a degree in communications, but I wanted to go into restaurant management. I had a few friends and family who helped keep me afloat, but I tended to lose people just as quickly as I'd found them. I wanted nothing more than to find something to give me hope--hope to continue fighting, hope that I'll accomplish more than my mental illness says I'm capable of.

My name is Clay Dabrowski, and this is my story.

I opened my deep, hazelnut eyes as the sound of my phone alarm rang in my ears. The loud, drawn out *beep, beep, beep* continued until I rolled over and slapped the phone in an effort to stop the noise. The noise ended, leaving only silence lingering in the room. I slung my legs off my black futon bed and sat up.

My brown hair reaching down to my ears that I normally wore parted to the right side of my face was now in shambles, looking like someone had taken a balloon and rubbed it against one side of my head. My bushy beard curled up to my lips. I spat and sputtered the hair away from my mouth. Sleep filled the corners of my eyes. I used my index finger to gently brush the corner of my eyes, freeing my blurry vision just a smidge.

As I stood, I arched my back to stretch my stiff muscles. I glanced down at my phone still sitting on the nightstand. It was 3:30 in the afternoon. I had slept all day again after I'd pulled an open-to-close shift the night before. I was the lead server, with aspirations to get into management at a local restaurant chain called *The Door*. I had been there for nearly four years now, where

I'd started as a server and worked my way into head server, and finally management now that I was twenty-one. I was set to start management training in a week, but for now remained the head server.

I had to be at work in an hour and a half. I debated calling in sick; I would much rather be going out on the town with my best friend Luke on a Friday night. I made my way to the bathroom to begin my morning--or rather afternoon--regime to get ready. Once I had brushed my teeth and turned on the shower, I finally decided not to call out. I needed the money more than anything. After all, I had student loans to pay.

I finished getting dressed and made my way out of my second-story apartment. I walked to the edge of the railing and looked down at the cone my neighbor had stolen with the sign "Parking for I25 ONLY" typed across a laminated piece of paper glued to the cone. I chuckled to myself as I made my way down the steps to my deep, sea blue Challenger, glimmering in the sun from the small metallic flakes in the paint. This car was my pride and joy. It's what I had saved up for and what I wanted my entire life. I'd made the leap and finally bought it after my most recent birthday. Since then, I had made several modifications to the car: new exhaust, upgraded manifolds, racing tuned, window louvres, and tint. It was mine that was for sure. Young and dumb I was.

As I got in the car, I slid the keys into the ignition. The car *ding, ding, dinged* as it woke from its slumber. I slowly turned the key, bringing the roar of the engine to life. The sound filled the empty apartment complex with a loud lion's roar. I smiled. I loved the sound of the engine roaring to life, the deep throaty growl of the exhaust and engine combining into one.

Driving was one of my happy places. The sound of the engine would soothe me, causing me to get lost in thought. Most of the time I would ride with the radio off, my mind wandering as I took in the sounds of the car. It was where I went to escape life.

I pulled into the parking lot and into a spot closest to the employee entrance at the back of the restaurant. As I put the car in park, I closed my eyes, leaned my head back against the headrest of my seat, and listened to the sound of the engine growling. "I don't want to be here," I thought to myself as I sighed.

I opened my eyes and turned to scan the employee parking lot to see who I'd be working with. There was only one vehicle I didn't recognize. I couldn't think of a single person I worked with who drove a champagne-colored minivan. I scratched my head as I racked my brain for who it might have been, but to no avail. "It must be a new hire for the kitchen or hostess," I said to myself.

I slowly opened my car door as a flood of sunlight broke the plain of my tinted windows. I squinted as I stood and shielded my eyes. The horn honked as I pressed the key fob on my walk to the employee door, opening it and feeling the cool breeze of the A/C hit me in the face.

I glanced over to my right where the computer was and saw Ma sitting there. Ma was like everyone's work mother. She was there for us when we needed her, gave us motherly advice, even fed us. She had no kids of her own, but she gave a special kind of love to all the young servers and cooks who came through the doors of *The Door*. She sported pixie cut blonde hair and was slightly taller than I was. She wore her all-black work uniform and server's apron.

"Hey, Ma," I started before glancing around her into the office. What I saw made me stop in mid-sentence. I reached up and slowly placed my index finger and middle finger against my neck to check my pulse and make sure I hadn't died and gone to Heaven. "Who is that?" I finally asked, nodding towards the office.

Standing in the office, assumingly filling out new hire documents, was the most beautiful girl I had ever laid my eyes on. There she was, her magnificent red hair shining in the dull lights of the office. She was a bit shorter than me, clad in the black uniform. She was gorgeous. Who was she? Was she the one driving the minivan?

Ma turned around to see who I was talking about, "That's the new hostess. She knows Rita. Why?"

"She's gorgeous, Ma." I couldn't help but stare at her.

"Clay, haven't you learned your lesson about messing with girls here?" Ma shook her head and stood up. "Be careful, Clay. I just don't want to see you get hurt. Again."

Ignoring her warning, I moved past her and made my way into the office to introduce myself. I didn't want to be too obvious about it though. I didn't want to come off too strong and give off a stalker vibe.

"Hey, Peter." I walked through the door and looked at the manager assisting the new angel with her paperwork. "Who's this?" I asked before realizing I'd just done what I was hoping to avoid.

The girl turned around, the most beautiful smile painted across her face, highlighted by her freckles shimmering like tiny stars surrounding her crescent moon-like smile. My gaze met her golden-brown eyes shining like coins in the midday sunlight. Was it just me, or did she stare back at me with the same intensity?

"I'm Bailey. Bailey Childe," she smiled, extending her hand towards me.

I reached out to grab her hand carefully. The feeling of her soft skin gave me goosebumps. Her hand fit perfectly into mine, causing my face to flush red. "Clay. Clay, uh, Clay Dabrowski," I stammered. That smile, painted perfectly by God's pink paintbrush, canvassed the bottom of her face and radiated joy into the air. "Nice to meet you."

"She's our newest hostess. She starts training with Rita tonight," chimed in Peter with his normal delayed fashion. "Clay's our head server and soon-to-be newest manager."

"Nice to meet you, Clay Uh." She giggled.

My face, once again, flushed red.

"**G**ood evening, my name is Clay, and I'll be your server today," I began as I introduced myself to my first table of the night. "Our special is the filet mignon served with an asparagus and parmesan sauce. For drinks, we have Patron margaritas for $8.99. What can I get y'all started with for drinks and an appetizer?" As I finished my spiel and jotted down the table's drink order, I made my way to the kitchen.

Approaching the kitchen door, I turned to see Bailey standing at the hostess stand. She was gorgeous, her long red hair twisting and turning down her back and sneaking across her shoulders. Her radiant smile pressed her lips up when a guest entered, and the way her eyes lit up the dark room had me enthralled in her beauty.

I pushed my way through the kitchen door to finish fulfilling my table's order.

"Clay," a voice called out from behind me.

I turned around to see Ma coming through the kitchen door on my heels. "Yes, Ma?"

"I saw the way you were looking at her."

"Ma, there's something different about her. I just know it. She's the type of girl I could see myself marrying in the future."

"Clay, you barely know her. I get it; she's a beautiful girl, but you don't know anything else about her. She could be even more crazy than Morgan was, and you know how badly that ended. I still think you should have ended up with Ms. Marissa."

"Marissa and I were just not compatible. You know that. And I highly doubt Bailey is as crazy as Morgan was. That one will be hard to beat. You always tell me to trust the Lord, that he will give me the signs when I meet 'The One'. What if this is my sign? This feeling I have--it could be that sign."

Ma was extremely religious, and consistently preached to me about looking for signs and trusting God. I was at a stage in my life where I was on the fence with religion, but I knew how important it was to her. I respected that.

"Clay, Clay, Clay," Ma sighed, shaking her head. "Honey, I know you. You're a hopeless romantic. You want to find love. I want you to find love. You've got to look outside of this place though. You're stuck here fifty, sixty hours a week, and all you see are the girls in here. You need to look elsewhere."

"Look," I sighed, glancing at her with pleaful eyes. "I just finally found the right combination of medicine to keep my bipolar under control. I'm happy, in ways I have never felt before. I can finally see a light at the end of this tunnel. I think she could be that light. This is a new chapter in my life, and it starts with meeting her."

"Clay, please be careful honey. Please."

"Ma, I will. Just," I paused, struggling to find the right words to explain to her this feeling. "Just trust me on this one." I finished pouring the drinks for my table. I made my way out to the dining room to see more tables had been filled. It was going to be a long Friday night.

As the night wound down and the restaurant cleared out, I seized the opportunity to go talk to Bailey once again and quickly made my way to where she and Rita stood. Bailey appeared exhausted, her hair a stringy mess, sweat beading on her forehead, and pure exhaustion filled her eyes, yet she was still beautiful. I could only imagine how I looked.

I walked to the stand and glanced over at the seating chart sprawled across the surface. "Hello, Clay." Bailey smiled.

"Oh, hey. Bailey, right?" I asked, trying to fake not knowing who she was like I hadn't been thinking about her all night.

"Yes, sir."

"How has your first night gone?" I asked nonchalantly as I made my way to one of the seats in the lobby. Bailey followed and sat down beside me.

"It was really good. Is it always this busy on a Friday night? I couldn't keep the tables clean enough for Rita to seat people." She laughed.

"Always. Always like that on Fridays. It gets crazy in here some-times. I'm just glad you were here to help clean tables as they emptied. Things wouldn't have gone as smoothly if you weren't here." I smiled softly at her, hoping she would appreciate my compliment.

Her face flushed red as she looked down at the floor. "Thank you, Clay. Hey, I like your shoes," she giggled, pointing at my black non-slip work shoes.

Suddenly wishing that I had worn a nicer pair of shoes, I looked down at my now dirty shoes. "Oh yeah?"

"Yeah, I bet you wear those to school too, don't you?" she teased, adding a wink at the end of her sentence.

"Actually, I did when I was in college," I laughed. "Look, I hate buying shoes. So I only have this pair and one other pair. It's a lot easier to wear these to school and leave straight from there to work instead of going home.

"Speaking of school, are you in school, Bailey? High school? College?" I didn't truly think she was in high school, but you could never be too careful. Even if she was in high school though, we didn't hire anybody under eighteen so she was at least an adult.

"Yeah, I go to school in Spartanburg at Converse College," she smiled. My heart dropped as I heard the words come out of her mouth. Spartanburg was almost four hours from my coastal town of Myrtle Beach, South Carolina. The girl of my dreams, the most beautiful angel I had ever seen, would be moving four hours away in a matter of months.

Peter approached us, raising one brow as he looked at me sitting next to the new hostess. "Your cut Bailey," he said as he got to us.

Bailey glanced over at me and then back to Peter, blinking her eyes a few times. "It's restaurant talk for your shift is over." I laughed, nudging her playfully. "Have Rita show you what to do after you're cut, and you can go home."

"Okay, thank you!" She smiled as she stood up to make her way to where Rita was waiting.

"Oh, Bailey. Don't forget you get a free meal tonight for your first night training," I called out as I watched her walk away, biting my lip. "Just come see me when you're done, and I'll get it ordered for you." I smiled, not wanting to let go of the connection we had just built.

"Oh I will. I'm starving!" She turned to flash me another one of her heart stopping smiles before disappearing into the back of the restaurant.

As she walked away, I turned my attention to Rita, standing there with a smile on her face. "What?" I pointedly asked.

"You two," she said, nodding towards Bailey. "I haven't seen her smile or laugh like that, well, ever."

"She sure is something else." My gaze never left Bailey.

"**C**lay!" Bailey called out. She made her way across the restaurant towards me, waving her hand. "I think I'm done."

I looked over at her with a gentle smile. "Whatcha want to eat?"

"I don't know," she answered honestly. "Order me your favorite thing!"

"My favorite thing?" I chuckled. "Alright. I'm just going to warn you, I have weird tastes. How about a burger with peanut butter and bacon?" Bailey's face said it all when she scrunched up her nose, pursed her lips, and furrowed her brows. "Okay, not that then. What about the honey chicken mac and cheese?"

This time, her eyes lit up. "That sounds good!"

"Alright. Pick a seat in my section and I'll get it ordered for you. Got a drink?"

"I don't. Sweet tea?"

"Coming right up," I smiled as I walked past her to the kitchen. She made her way to a table in the furthest corner of my section.

A few minutes later, I returned with a sweet tea and a large green and white bowl filled to the brim with delicious mac and cheese and golden honey chicken. "Clay! This looks delicious!" she said as she unrolled her napkin and got ready to dive into her food.

"Thanks, I made it myself."

"Really?"

"No," I laughed as I turned and walked away. I couldn't help but to smile. Her voice sang to me in ways I had never been sung to before. I got to the server's station and printed out her receipt, scribbling away on it.

"What are you doing?" I heard Ma ask as she appeared by my side.

I quickly covered the receipt, stuffing it back into my server's apron. "Nothing."

"Uh-huh, don't forget, mommas know everything. You were doing a little more than nothing Clay." Man she was good.

"I was just doodling," I reached up and scratched the back of my head out of nervousness.

She gave me that glare that all moms had. The one that tells you she knows you're lying, but she trusts you to make the right decision. "Be careful, Clay."

I glanced over at Bailey's table and then turned my attention back to Ma. "I will be, I promise. I need to make my rounds." I left the station and began visiting my tables.

As she finished her final few bites, I made my way back over to Bailey. My heart began to pound within my chest. *Badum, badum, badum* it echoed. My hands became clammy as I reached into my apron to pull out a folded over receipt. I crinkled the receipt between my fingers as the nervousness crept through every crack and crevice of my body. The closer I got, the harder my heart pounded. "Just hand it to her, Clay." I told myself as I approached the table.

"Here you go Bailey, your total comes out to free dollars," I half-heartedly joked as I laid the folded receipt on the table and took the rest of the dishes from her table.

When Bailey unfolded the paper, she found my number scribbled across the top of the receipt with the words 'don't be afraid to use this' underneath the digits. I caught a glimpse of a brief smile creep onto her face as I walked away.

As the night drew on, I kept checking my phone. I would check nearly every ten minutes in hopes I'd see a message from Bailey. Finally, I pulled the smartphone out of my back pocket and this time the screen lit up. There was one new message from an unknown number.

I unlocked the phone, quickly pulling up the message. *Hey, it's Bailey :)* I couldn't help smiling to myself as I stared down at the screen. My heart skipped a beat

"What's got you smiling over there, Clay?" Peter said as he walked up to where I was leaning against the wall.

My smile grew. "Nothing, Peter. Nothing at all."

"It's the hostess, isn't it?" He side eyed me as he leaned against the wall beside me.

"It is." I trusted Peter enough to open up to him about this; he was the one manager who had respected me from day one and treated me as an equal when I'd decided I wanted to transition into management.

"Just be careful, Clay. You're going to be a manager now."

"I know. I'm taking it one day at a time." I said, texting Bailey back with an overly enthusiastic *Hey!*

A few days had passed since I'd met Bailey. She had used my number, probably against her better judgement.

"So tell me, what is your favorite food?" I had asked her. One of the must knows of a relationship.

"Mmmm pasta and chicken. I could eat either of those anytime."

"Good choice, mine is Italian food. We're going to get along just fine." I smiled as I sent the message, my heart building for her. *"What foods don't you like?"*

"I don't like pie, fruit shouldn't be hot. I don't like tomatoes or stuffing either."

"Oh no Bailey," I sent, teasing her. *"Pie is a must for me."*

"Guess that just means more pie for you, doesn't it? :)" I smiled at her text. My heart fluttered a little. *"Favorite color?"*

I chuckled to myself. *"Fun fact: I'm colorblind. But blue would be my favorite color of the ones I see."*

"OMG are you kidding?"

"Nope!"

I'd learned a lot of little things about her since we'd started talking and was growing attached to her personality, the kindness in her words, the innocence of her jokes, and the careful use of the words she chose.

2
Not a Date

I couldn't stop thinking about her; she was in my every dream. I slowly opened my eyes and rolled over to check my phone. It was noon, but more importantly I had a message from Bailey that read "*Good morning!*".

We had made plans to hang out the next night, the only day we both had off. We'd been athletes in high school and enjoyed the workout and team building that came with sports. It was a common ground on which we could connect.

She was a soccer player, even playing for her college's team. I, on the other hand, played baseball. Well, I attempted to be a baseball player. We had compromised and decided we would teach one another our chosen sport. Our plan was to go to the local batting cages and then to the local rec park to play soccer. I knew this wasn't a date, but I still felt nervous about hanging out with her.

As I got up from my bed and made my way into the bathroom for my mid-day routine, I heard a knock at my door. Before I could even open it, the door swung open. My best friend Luke Baldwin's husky frame stood before me. He adjusted his camo hat, his mullet tucked behind his ears. He ran a hand smoothly through his beard as he walked into my apartment and to the fridge to grab a cold beer. Typical Luke, my house was his house.

He turned to face me, making sure to look down. He wasn't much taller, but it mattered to him. "Me, you, bonfire at my house tomorrow night. Gonna have a few people over. Drink some beer. Play some pong. Might even put a tarp in the back of the truck and fill it with water to make our own pool."

"I can't make it buddy," I said, trying to be as vague as possible. "I, uh, got plans."

"I know that hesitation." Luke smiled, putting his hand on my shoulder. "You got a date, don't ya? Well, tell me about her. Come on now." Luke pulled me towards the living room where we plopped down on the couch. "Spit it out."

"Look," I started, choosing my next words carefully. "Her name is Bailey. She's a new hostess at The Door-"

"Man, I do not miss working crazy schedules at that place. I don't know how you still do it, Clay. It was stressful for me." Luke and I had met at The Door, Luke being a cook and me a server. Luke had moved onto another job a few weeks ago with Myrtle Beach Electric Authority.

"I know you don't," I chucked back before beginning again. "So, Bailey. I don't want people knowing we're hanging out - and it is not a date, Luke - because I could get in serious trouble now that I'm almost a manager. But dude, she is gorgeous!

She has these golden-brown eyes that look into your soul. It's like she knows all my problems and all my struggles already. Her smile shines like the moon in a midnight sky. Her hair is a crimson red that reminds me of a summer bonfire."

"So... She's your dream girl?""YES!" I shouted, standing up and slapping my friend on the back. "So, if you have anybody over from The Door, do NOT mention where I am. Please. It is not a date. I'm trusting you with this. As my best friend, I am begging you not to tell anyone."

"You got my word, man. I got you. You know that."

Bailey and I had texted all day, really trying to get to know one another. We started off by playing Twenty Questions, which wound up being fifty plus questions. I loved learning the little things about her. That her orite flower is the sunflower. We connected on having a stepdad who cared for us like we were their own. We connected on our love for family.

I looked down at my phone to see a message waiting for me that read, "*Your turn :)*". I smiled as I thought about my next question. Then it came to me, a question that I had been longing to ask since we met. I knew I shouldn't, but I couldn't wait until I got to work to ask it. I foolishly grabbed my phone in one hand and began typing.

"*So, do you have a boyfriend? Married? Engaged?*"

I kept my phone in one hand eagerly awaiting the text back, however I almost wished I hadn't when the reply came through. *"Not married, not engaged, but I do have a boyfriend,"* she sent. *"Is that okay? Can we still hang out tomorrow?"*

My heart sank. My dream girl was not only leaving in a few months, but she also had a boyfriend. How did I always find myself in situations like this? *"Of course it is! It's not like we're going on a date tomorrow lol."* I was not actually laughing out loud.

The next day, I sat on the couch with my roommate Brian as I eagerly waited for five to come around when I was supposed to be picking up Bailey. Brian was also a manager at *The Door* but at another location. He was smaller than me, both in weight and height, and his shaved head reminded me of someone who had recently come out of the army.

"Brian?" I blurted out.

"Yeah, man? What's up?"

"You and Janet met at The Door, right? How are you guys doing now that she's serving and you're managing? Like, do people judge you for it?"

"That's why I transferred stores. I had to. The owners made me. I couldn't date an employee working for me. Too many liabilities there they don't want to put up with. Why?" Brian asked, before pausing. "It's that damn redhead, isn't it? Man, be careful. You've been screwed over by a lot of girls in that place."

How did he know about Bailey? Oh, yeah. Janet probably blabbed to him about it. "Nah man, I was just curious how that worked for you guys. I forgot we even had a redhead working with us," I laughed, nervously.

"Don't bullshit me, Clay," Brian retorted, reaching over to playfully slap my arm. "Your dream girl has always been a redhead. Think I forgot about Marissa?"

How did everyone know my dream girl is a redhead? And why the hell did people keep going back to Marissa? "Come on man, I'm really just curious about you guys. Y'all have been together for a while and seem really happy. Just trying to find my own Janet out there." I turned my attention back to the TV, hoping that Brian would let go of the conversation.

As I got ready to hang out with Bailey, I started to spray on some of my best cologne. "Dumbass, you're going to do physical activities," I mumbled to myself. I looked down at the outfit I had picked out: a pair of dark blue jeans and a black polo shirt. I had overdressed big time.

I went and changed into something more suitable for our activities: a pair of athletic pants and my favorite blue t-shirt that read 'Your Ego Is Not Your Amigo'. I made my way out of my room and headed to the door, hoping to avoid Brian and another awkward conversation.

"Clay, you're wearing that on a date?" Brian turned around on the couch to catch me trying to sneak out.

I rolled my eyes. "I'm not going on a date, Brian."

He laughed. "Yeah, sure. And I'm not going to have sex with Janet tonight."

Dick. "I'm really not, I'm just going to hang out with Bail-"

Before I could catch myself, Brian stood up and shouted "I knew it! I fucking knew it! You're going out with that redhead tonight. Bailey, right? Man, I am good!" He laughed, now jumping on the couch in excitement. "My man has a date tonight! It's been six months since you and a girl... you know. But seriously, what's with the outfit?"

I was frustrated that I had just outed myself but was becoming even more frustrated with Brian's gloating. "Man, please don't say anything to anybody. We aren't going on a date, honest. She already has a boyfriend anyways. We are just going to hang out. I'm taking her to the batting cages and then she's gonna take me to the park to learn how to play soccer. Don't make a big deal out of it," I said, pleading to my friend.

"Relax," Brian said as he returned to a sitting position on the couch, throwing his hand up with his index and middle finger pointed at the ceiling. "Scout's Honor, I won't say a word. Well, maybe to Janet."

"Brian..."

"You know she won't tell anyone. She didn't tell anyone about your other work flings, did she?" He was right. She had seen me with several different servers and hostesses from work when I was serving and never said anything. Ma was right; I worked way too much. Now that I was going to be her manager though...

"Yeah, you're right," I said, making my way to the door to finally escape my interrogation session with Brian.

Bailey had requested I pick her up in the parking lot of the supermarket across from *The Door*. I wasn't quite sure why I couldn't just pick her up from her house, but I gladly obliged. As long as I was getting to hang out with her, I really didn't care.

As I sat in my Challenger, the engine slowly rumbling, I saw the champagne colored minivan pull into the spot beside me. I looked over and smiled as I spotted Bailey waving at me while unbuckling her seatbelt. She hopped out of the driver's side door and made her way into the passenger seat of my car.

"Your car is beautiful!" she exclaimed, closing the door and looking at me with beaming eyes,

She looked even more beautiful tonight. Her hair was put up in a ponytail. She had a little makeup accenting her features, her freckles still peeking through. Her eyes shone bright like the night sky. She had on a purple tank top that fit her form like a glove. The same feeling I had when I first saw her worked its way back through my body. I shivered as I felt goosebumps sprouting up on my arms. "You look beautiful," I blurted out without thinking. *Why did you say that?*

"Why thank you, Clay," she said, blushing and looking down. "You look quite handsome yourself."

I couldn't help but stare at her. How was it that one human being could be so amazingly gorgeous? She was perfect in every meaning of the word. Every twist and turn of her body gave you new hope and desires and left you yearning for more. I shifted my car into reverse and headed towards the batting cages.

"Tell me about your boyfriend," I uttered.

Bailey looked over at me with a sad smile sprawled across her otherwise perfect face. "He's been my best friend for a long time. We just started dating about a year ago. But..."

"But?"

"But it feels one sided. He doesn't drive, so he hasn't come to see me at school. I haven't seen him since I've been home for summer. I just want someone who will give 100% and will do for me what I do for them."

"Bailey, I can tell you that you most certainly deserve that. I know I've only known you for a few days now, but you have one of the most kind and pure personalities of anybody I have ever met. You *do* deserve someone who is going to treat you just as good, if not better, than you treat them. I'm sorry you aren't getting that, but you should really talk to him, give him the chance to change."

There was so much more I wanted to say to her. I wanted to tell her I would take her in my arms and hold her close like she deserved. I wanted to be the reason she smiled at night before she went to sleep. I wanted to be the person that treated her right.

Bailey sat in silence until we pulled into the parking lot by the batting cages. "You're right. I do deserve that, and he deserves my honesty and communication on this, too."

We piled out of the car and made our way to the front desk where I got enough tokens for us to each have five turns in the cages. "Will you show me how to do it first?" Bailey asked.

I turned to her, a smile forming on my face. "I'm not the best, but I'll show you the best I can." I slid the black batting helmet over my head and made my way into the cage.

I slipped my token into the machine and stood in the batter's box.

Don't screw this up Clay, I thought to myself. *She's watching you. Show her what you can do. But what if you can't do enough?*

WHOOSH! The baseball left the machine flying past me and into the strike zone behind me. *Shit.*

I focused my attention back on the machine. I watched as the mechanical arm made its way back around, scooping up a ball, and then sending it flying out the middle towards the zone. I leaned back, pushing my hips forward as I lifted the bat off my shoulder, and swung it through the strike zone as I twisted my front foot.

DING! The aluminum bat connected with the ball, sending it in the air and towards the back of the cage.

Behind me, Bailey started clapping. "Impressive."

I continued hitting the ball, making solid contact with the remaining eight pitches. As I finished, I slid my helmet off and walked out of the cage, passing the helmet to Bailey. "You're up."

Bailey slipped the helmet on her head, her red mane falling out the sides and back of it. She stared at me, hunger in her eyes. Her breathing quickened as a nervous look overcame her face. I reached out and brushed the hair from around her shoulders to behind her back. I moved the stray hairs falling on her face and tucked them into the helmet. Her eyelashes fluttered as my skin traced across hers and a small smile appeared.

She stepped into the batting cages, and I followed behind her. "Okay, first step in that box," I said pointing at the white square drawn on the concrete. "Spread your feet apart and line them up with your shoulders. Bend your knees slightly, just enough for a little bounce. Hold the bat like this." I positioned her hands properly, left hand on the bottom, slightly touching the knob of the bat, and her right hand resting just above the other. My hand brushing against hers sent goosebumps up my arm.

"Good, you want to keep your hands like this. Now let the bat hover over your shoulder. Once the ball leaves the machine, take a small step out with your front foot. Now, in one quick motion, rotate your hips to create momentum for the swing. Turn your shoulders into the swing, plant your front foot, and pretend you're squishing a bug."

"Squishing a bug?" she laughed. "Got it."

I popped a token into the machine and made my way out of the cages. "You got this!" I cheered. The first ball left the machine's mechanical arm and zoomed past Bailey. "That's alright, now you're ready!"

She turned to me with excitement in her eyes and a smile on her face. She turned back around, watching the machine throw the next ball. With a long swing, she whiffed and missed the ball. Instead of being upset, a laugh emitted from her lips. "This is fun!"

I smiled at her happiness. She really was something special. Despite the struggles she faced with hitting the ball, she was having fun. She just enjoyed life, which was something I wanted to learn how to do for myself. I hoped I would have the opportunity for her to teach me just how to do it.

After a few more swings, she finally made contact with one sending it dribbling in front of her.

"You did it!" I shouted and began clapping my hands. "Now do that again!" And with the next pitch, she made contact again. And again. As the last of our tokens were eaten by the machine, we packed up and headed back to the car.

"How about some food before we go to the soccer field?" I asked, opening her door and swaying my arm inward.

"I'm starving," Bailey moaned as she got in the car.

We sat in a booth tucked away in a corner of a local burger joint, waiting for our food as we talked and got to know one another better. I instantly felt comfortable with her, open even. I had shut myself off from everyone years ago after my high school girlfriend had cheated on me with over twenty people, rejecting letting anyone get close to me. I had flings here and there and some girlfriends that bordered on becoming serious, but I'd always screwed it up somehow. I'd never wanted to open up to them. I had been afraid they would see me as a monster and ultimately leave me hurt again. With her, though, I wanted to tell her all my secrets.

"When I was a kid," I started. "I didn't have a home when I stayed with my dad, and I use that term very loosely. We stayed in hotel rooms and cars, aunt's and uncle's houses, even parking lots. It was hard not knowing where I was going to lay my head down at night. Sometimes, we would sleep on those cold, hard plastic benches outside of businesses."

Bailey looked at me, not with fear but with genuine care and hurt in her eyes. She wasn't scared of my past, and she wasn't hurt by my confession. She hurt *for* me. She wanted to comfort me from my past. "When did things get better for you, Clay? That's something I would never wish on anyone."

"I was about seven," I started. "My younger brother was five, so he doesn't have much of a recollection from then. I do. It's something that eats away at me every day. But it's something that made me stronger, it showed me I could face anything and come out on top."

Bailey gave me a sad smile as her eyes searched the pain in my eyes. "I'm so glad you haven't let it tear you down Clay. You're one of the strongest people I know for that."

"But enough about me and this dreary subject. Who is your favorite soccer player?" I asked, shifting in my seat and changing the subject from the dreary topic I had mistakenly picked.

"Ahh I would have to say Hope Solo!" She exclaimed ecstatically.

I had no idea who that was, so I went with the joke approach. "Is she Han Solo's brother?"

"I don't think so, but they may be related. He's in Aerosmith, isn't he?" She asked, in the most serious tone.

I couldn't help but laugh. I felt bad about laughing, but I couldn't help myself. She arched her eyebrow and cocked her head as I looked up at her. "I take it you've never seen Star Wars?" I finally asked.

"Han Solo is from Star Wars. Right. I haven't ever seen them, but I should have known that," she laughed back. Her laugh was mesmerizing. It was unrestrained and free, with so much joy behind it. Even if we couldn't date, she would quickly become one of my best friends, of that I was sure.

A

fter dinner, we headed to the rec field to play soccer. We pulled into the parking lot of the soccer fields, and I turned my car off, looking over at Bailey. "You ready?"

"I am," she started. "But the real question is, are you?"

I chuckled softly, because I honestly wasn't. "Well, there's only one way to find out, isn't there?"

We trudged out to the middle of the soccer field where Bailey laid down the soccer ball. "Okay, first things first: Controlling the ball. You don't want to put too much force behind the ball. You still want to keep it in front of you so that you can make a move in an instant if a defender is coming at you. As you're passing it from foot to foot, use the inside of your foot for the best control."

I started dribbling the ball back and forth between my feet, moving up and down the soccer field to practice. I wasn't very good. I couldn't keep control of the ball, and it kept rolling away or going the opposite direction I wanted it to. I was getting embarrassed, but I was still having fun with Bailey cheering me on.

"You're doing great, Clay! Now we're going to practice kicking the ball. Bend your knees slightly. Are you right or left-handed?"

"Right." My heartbeat quickened as I began processing the information. I was nervous, I didn't want to embarrass myself, but the way she stared at me was magical.

"Good, lets focus on kicking with that foot then. I'm going to put the ball here. I want you to stand in front of it and take three steps back and three steps to the left. Focus on the lower side of the ball, closest to the ground. Keep your eye on that spot. When you make contact, lock your ankle, and kick it with the laces." She looked beautiful talking about what she loved. Her eyes sparkled and an excited smile lit up her face. Her purple tank top was a couple of shades darker from sweat, but she was still as beautiful as she had been when I picked her up.

"Kick with the laces, got it." I ran forward and reared back my foot, putting all of my power into a kick. My foot missed the ball completely, sending me backwards and onto my back. I heard Bailey giggling as I lay there, embarrassed in the wet grass. "Did I get it?" I asked jokingly as I pulled myself off the ground.

"Not quite, champ." Bailey laughed pointing at the ball.

I prepared myself again, remembering what Bailey had told me. I reared back, sending the laces of my shoes into the ball. The ball slowly rolled forward - not very far, but it did move.

"You did it!" Bailey called out. "Now, let's play. I'll protect the goal, and you try to score."

"Oh wow, you really want to embarrass me, don't you?"

"I won't embarrass you. You'll probably embarrass yourself." She laughed as she turned to walk to the goal on the far end of the field. Once she got there she turned around, cupping her hands around her mouth and yelled. "Okay! I'm ready."

I took a deep breath and started moving the ball with my foot. I inched up the field slowly, careful not to lose my footing on the ball. As I got closer, Bailey ran out of the goal towards me. I reared back and connected the lace of my shoes with the ball, sending it to the opposite side of the goal from Bailey, rolling into the net.

"I did it!" I yelled out as she continued to run at me. "Bailey, what're you doing?" She wasn't stopping. She had a maniacal smile spread across her lips. She got closer to me, playfully tackling me to the ground. We rolled around the grass before I rolled her on her back and held her arms down. My legs straddled her stomach as I looked down at her, my hands wrapped softly around her wrists.

I stared down at her, deep into her eyes. Her gaze caught mine, and we locked, reading each other's souls like they were open books. I wanted to tell her my every secret and hear every one of hers. To take away any pain she may have and stop those who were hurting her. I wanted to let her into my life. I wanted her.

My head began to lower, my nose hovering above hers. I looked down at her lips then back at her eyes. "We can't!" We both said at the same time as I lifted myself off the ground and extended my hand to help her up.

We couldn't. But we wanted to.

I laid in bed that night, tossing and turning from restless thoughts. That night had been one of the best nights of my life. Getting to know her and being in her presence was all I could have ever dreamed of and then some. But the lingering thought that she was taken nipped in the back of my mind. Everything about her felt so right to me, yet she wasn't mine. I wasn't hers. We weren't each other's.

I wouldn't ask her to leave him for me. I couldn't do that. That was selfish, and I cared too much about her feelings. If she was happy, I was happy. She was quickly becoming my best friend as well. And if all we turned out to be was best friends, I would be okay with that, too. She was that kind of amazing.

It Started with a Kiss in a Challenger

A few weeks passed since Bailey and I had hung out. We remained close friends, hanging out and having fun. We would grab dinner and talk about our days. I was there for her when she needed me, and she was there for me when I needed her. Nothing had happened since the first time we'd hung out; we just became friends. Best friends.

I was on my way to pick up Bailey when my phone rang. On the screen flashed her name. I pressed the phone button on my steering wheel. "Hello."

Sobs came from the other end of the phone, long sobs that tore at my heart strings and made my stomach turn knots. "Clay, where are you?" She sniffled out.

"I'm on my way to pick you up, I'll be there in about five. What's going on, Bailey?"

"Clay, Blake and I broke up."

"Bailey," I started, carefully debating my next words. "I'm so sorry, I'll be there soon."

As I hung up the phone, I sped up a little bit more. I wanted to be there for her as soon as possible. I wanted to give her a shoulder to cry on. Knowing my best friend was hurting was heartbreaking. The feelings overwhelmed me for some reason. I just couldn't seem to shake them.

I pulled into the supermarket parking lot that had become our regular meeting place. I put the car in park and pulled the keys out almost simultaneously. I leapt out the car and to her door, where she was already opening the door and falling into my arms.

I wrapped an arm around her shoulders, pulling her head closely into my chest. "Let it out. I'm here," I said as I rested the side of my face on her head.

Her sobs went on and on. She finally glanced up at me. "It isn't like I only lost a boyfriend of year, but I feel like I've lost my best friend in the process."

I arched an eyebrow. "What do you mean?"

She looked back down and sniffled. "We've been best friends since we were four years old. We've known each other that long. Things will never be the same between us." I squeezed her a little more, wanting nothing more than to take her pain and pull it from her

She was finally able to gain her composure. She sniffled a few times and looked up at me, fresh tears still glistening in the corner of her eyes, and whispered, "thank you."

"That's what friends are for," I said into the top of her head.

She backed away from me, brushing herself off, and wiping around her eyes. "Still want to go to dinner with a wreck like me?" She laughed, the last bit of tears being wiped away from her eyes.

"Bailey, I'll go with that wreck anywhere, anytime." I smiled as I grabbed her hand and led her to the passenger door.

I slid into the booth across from Bailey in the small diner. The place brought you back to the fifties with its shimmering metal interior and black and white checkered floors. One of the best places in town to get a burger and a shake, and it had quickly become one of our favorite places to grab a bite to eat.

Inevitably, the breakup came up in conversation. "He wasn't there anymore," she said, placing her menu down and looking at me.

"What do you mean?" I lowered my menu, my gaze meeting hers. I saw the hurt and pain still swimming inside of her.

"I was the only one putting in effort. He would never come see me at school. He hardly talked to me, and he just seemed disinterested. I deserve better than that, don't I?"

I reached across the table, taking her hands in mine, and looking into her eyes. "Bailey, you deserve happiness and then some. You deserve to be able to smile everyday knowing you're loved. You deserve someone who is going to go see you, who yearns to be in your presence. You deserve it all."

She looked down at her hands in mine, her fingers lightly brushing the inside of my palm as the words I spoke ran through her mind. She finally looked up at me, her eyes glistening in the dinner's fluorescent lights. "Clay, you are my best friend, you know that?"

I smiled, feeling the heat building up in my cheeks as a rush of red took over. "Bailey, honestly I just want to see you happy. We've become so close over the last few weeks, really gotten to know one another, and from what I know you deserve happiness."

I could feel the tips of her fingers curling around my hands, the light embrace sending firework sensations through every nerve in my body. We stared into each other's eyes, learning and yearning for more. I carefully bit the corner of my lip, holding back the smile erupting from within. I looked away before the red could completely consume my face.

"Clay," Bailey began before the server appeared at our table side, handing out our food and extra refills.

I sat, anxiously waiting for what she was going to say next. After an awkward silence, I spoke up, "Yes Bailey?"

She jumped slightly in her seat, repositioning herself in the midst. "I was," she paused for a moment, glancing out the window and back to me. "I was just going to ask how much longer you thought the food might be." The weak smile following her sentence confirmed that was far from the truth, but I decided to let it go for the time being. Besides, she had a lot on her mind, and I wasn't trying to pry and bring up more hurt.

Not much more was said about Blake during the rest of the meal or our time together. I knew it was still a fresh wound and one I didn't want to throw salt onto. She knew I would be there for her however she needed me and knowing that made me feel a little bit better. We pulled back into the parking lot next to her minivan. I looked over at her, the side of her head pressed against the cold window. She was lost in thought, and I could only imagine the thoughts racing through her mind right now.

"Is there something wrong with me?" Bailey asked, taking her head off the window and shifting her body to face mine. "I mean, am I not worth the effort? Am I not worth a couple hours' drive every once and a while? I gave him my all, Clay. I gave him everything I could. He was my best friend for so long, and now things are different. I don't know if things will ever be the same between us." She sighed, closing her eyes to hold in her tears.

The pain in her voice, the hurt she swallowed with each word would have been enough to buckle my knees had we been standing up.

"Bailey, it isn't you. Sometimes, just because you're best friends, it doesn't necessarily translate into love. Some people are better off friends, some people are best friends and in love. Things happen, for whatever reason they may happen, and all we can do is learn from it. Take the pain and hurt, take the lessons we learned, and make ourselves better. Because eventually we're going to meet the one we're truly meant to be with, and it will all make sense. When that moment comes, we need to be as happy with ourselves as possible so they can be happy with us too." I explained the best I could.

Deafening silence filled the car, only the hum of the engine provided any background noise. I shifted my body, reaching down and taking her hands in mine again. It was amazing how well our hands fit together, how her simple touch warmed my body on the cool night. She must have been thinking the same thing as her eyes traveled from our hands to my eyes.

Like gravity forcing us together, we both inched our heads towards one another. I saw the want and desire in her eyes, her stare full of pure craving. I stared at her, burning my story into her mind. I loosened my grip on one of her hands, sliding my hand up her arm, tracing the edge of her neck, and gently placing it on her cheek.

My eyes closed, and I could only hope hers did as well. I leaned in, feeling for her touch with my lips until finally they met hers. The warmth of her lips radiated through mine, sending happiness radiating through my body. Our lips locked, her bottom lip in between mine as we paused.

I slid my hand from her cheek to the back of her head, pulling her in further for the embrace. Our lips still locked, pulling us closer together than we had ever been over the last several weeks.

I pulled back a tiny bit, leaving almost nothing in between us. I opened my eyes, my forehead resting against hers. Slowly, her eyes opened, her eyelashes fluttering like a butterfly's wing as she searched for my eyes. Once our gazes connected, a smile stole both of our expressions.

And then anxiety hit me. "I'm sorry," I said, pulling further away and looking out the window. "I shouldn't have done that. You just broke up with Blake. I shouldn't have done that."

"Hey," she said, reaching out and gently wrapping her hand around my forearm. "It wasn't just you. I made that decision, too. I don't regret it."

I looked over at her, unsure if she was telling me the truth or trying to make me feel better. But I could read the truth like the words were right before me. She meant every word she had just said, plus a whole lot more she hadn't.

Her eyes danced to the clock on my dash, reading 10:45 pm. "Shit, shit, shit," she clamored, gathering her bag and things from the passenger side floorboard. "I've got to get home. I told my parents I would be home by 10:30!"

She gathered the last of her things, hopping out of the car. She stopped and turned to me with her lip in between her teeth. "Thank you for tonight," she said, closing the door on her words.

I pulled into my apartment complex, bringing the car to a halt and taking away its life. I hadn't stopped smiling since I'd left Bailey. The kiss was better than I could ever have imagined—the way her lips tasted like sweet flowers, the sensations that lit up my body, it was the stuff dreams were made of. I wouldn't have been surprised if fireworks had been going off in the background.

As soon as my feet hit the sidewalk, I heard Brian calling out from the balcony above me. "What're you wearing that shit-eating smile for?"

Before I had a chance to respond, Janet stuck her head over the balcony and looked down at me, her stringy black hair hanging down from the balcony like the girl from The Ring. "I bet he went out with Bailey." She said.

I silently shook my head and rolled my eyes, locking my car and making my way up the stairs. When I got to the top, Brian offered me a beer, and Janet moved from her seat to Brian's lap.

"Yes, you two, it was Bailey," I started, sitting down and opening the beer. I pulled out a cigarette and lit it, needing a nicotine fix after the night I had just had. "She broke up with her boyfriend and..."

"You're smiling because she broke up with her boyfriend? You've been hanging out with Brian too much," Janet half-heartedly joked.

"Low blow, Janet. Low blow," Brian remarked, smirking at her before looking back at me. "So did you make your move?"

"I didn't mean to, and I wasn't going to." I started, shifting uncomfortably in my seat. "But we did kiss." Brian's eyes lit up as he looked at Janet, whose face was a bit more disapproving. "We didn't intend to. It just kind of happened in the heat of the moment."

Brian reached up, high fiving me for what he viewed as a win. I gave him a weak high five in return, causing him to come back at me with, "Why do you look so glum?"

"I just don't want her to think I took advantage of her being in such a bad state. She just broke up with her boyfriend, lost her best friend, and lo and behold I swoop in for the kiss. It's kind of messed up, isn't it?"

Janet was the first one to speak up. "Clay, did she push you away? Did she tell you to stop? Who kissed who first? And don't say you kissed each other, because that just isn't how it happens."

A smile returned to my face as I remembered the moment our lips met, the moment my night had changed completely, maybe even my life. "She didn't push me away, in fact I'm pretty sure she embraced it. I closed my eyes first, so I'm going to guess I kissed her first. She told me she didn't regret it, but what if she does tomorrow?"

Janet stood up, seeing the real concern in my voice, and shifted to a serious tone. "You're looking way too much into this, Clay. If you felt it was right, and she didn't give any indicators she regretted it, then don't worry about it. It sounds like this has been a long time coming. I see the way you two look at each other at The Door, pretending not to notice each other."

I looked up to Janet, puffing on the slow burning cigarette I held in between my teeth. "You think so?"

"I've seen a lot of work flings working there. You two are different. You two are special, believe that."

More Than Friends

I sat in the office of The Door as the clock struck closing time. It had been a long night, full of a lot of surprises. One customer took it upon themselves to tell their kid to shit on the floor, simply because her to-go-order didn't come out when she wanted. At first, I thought the bartender was joking, but as soon as I walked into the dining room, the smell that infiltrated my nose assured me he wasn't.

But of course, this would happen when I tried to wish the shift would go by faster. Why couldn't it be easy to get to the end of my shift? All I wanted was to see Bailey. Since we'd kissed last week, things hadn't really changed. We were still best friends, still hanging out regularly. She seemed happier since she'd broken up with Blake, and that made me happy.

My phone buzzed on the desk, causing me to look down. *"I have Chinese outside in case you're hungry."* the message from Bailey read. I couldn't help but smile at her kindness. I also knew that meant she was outside.

I hopped out of my chair, hurrying out the side door. I saw my car sitting under the sole streetlamp in the parking lot, and next to it was my favorite minivan. I hurried over to the spaces and made my way to the driver's side door of the van.

The window rolled down, revealing Bailey's stunning smile and beautiful freckled face. "Howdy there." She pulled out a brown paper bag filled with containers of Chinese food and handed it to me.

"Thank you for this," I said, holding up the container of food.

"I figured you might be hungry, and I knew you wouldn't feel like cooking when you got off work. Plus, maybe I'm being greedy, but I was hoping to have your full attention tonight. Now hurry, go finish closing," she laughed, rolling the window up.

Her parents were out of town, and she was coming over to hang out for the night. Her sister was still expecting her home at some point, but we had more leeway than before. While she was in college, she lived with her parents when she came home to visit, and naturally they had their rules. It was something I had come to accept, but I was excited to be able to spend more time with her.

I pulled into the parking lot of my apartment complex, Bailey's headlights shining bright in my rear-view mirror. She had never been to my apartment before, so I had driven extra careful on the way there so as not to lose her. I got out of the car, walked to hers, and opened her door for her.

"Well aren't you just the gentleman? I didn't even have to ride with you, and you still opened my door," she said, sliding out of her driver's seat.

She looked gorgeous in her minimal makeup, baggy grey sweatpants, and a navy blue sweatshirt covering her curves. I wrapped my arm around her shoulders, rubbing her arm as we walked to keep her warm. We got to the door, and I whispered to her, "Let me go in and make sure Brian and Janet aren't here."

I quietly unlocked the door and pushed it open, sticking my head in and looking around the dark apartment. I crept through the house, listening and looking for the pair. Finding no sign of them, I flipped the light switches on and let Bailey inside. I made my way into my room, grabbing a fresh change of clothes and turning the tv on for her. I handed her the remote and made my way to get changed.

I walked out of my room to head to the bathroom to change. Before I could get there, the front door opened and Brian and Janet's voices rang through the apartment. Shit. I quickly closed the bedroom door behind me before they could see in there.

"Hey guys," I said to them as they walked past my door, where I was awkwardly guarding.

"What're you hiding?" Brian asked.

"I'm not sure what you mean, buddy," I lied.

"There's someone in your room, isn't there?" Janet asked, a smile making its way onto her face. "Is it Bailey?"

I reached back, rubbing my neck. They knew. They were too good. "Yes, it is,"

"Oh la la." Brian wiggled his eyebrows.

"Hey, Bailey!" Janet shouted.

"Hi!" I heard Bailey's voice sing from behind the door. God, her voice was beautiful.

"Okay, that's enough. I'm going to get changed. Don't harass her, please."

"We won't. I promise," Janet said, grabbing Brian's shirt sleeve and dragging him away into the living room.

Something came over me while I was changing, something primal. I wanted her, all of her like I had in my dreams.

No. I couldn't. I respected her more than that. We weren't even technically dating yet; we were just friends. But I wanted to taste her lips in between mine again, and the thought of it consumed me.

I left the bathroom, leaving the clothes strung across the floor, and went into my bedroom. Bailey was laying instead of sitting on the bed now, her head propped up by her elbow. I licked my lips as I made my way to her, playfully rolling her over to her back and startling her. "Is this okay?" I asked her before I continued.

Her smile and lip bite, followed by a happy nod was the answer I was looking for. "Good, because I've been wanting to do this since our first time hanging out." I leaned down, my nose hovering above hers like the night we first hung out. Only this time, there was nothing stopping me.

My lips met hers, feeling the smooth curves filling in where mine left off. Her hands reached out, grabbing the side of my head and pulling me in deeper. The flowery scent of her perfume crept into my nose, filling it with her sweet smell. The taste of her lips lit my taste buds on fire.

I rolled to the side, rolling her with me, our lips still locked. I pulled my head back slightly and opened my eyes. She was looking back, the corner of her lip tucked in.

"Bailey Childe, will you be my girlfriend?" I whispered to her, my breath beating down on her ear.

"Yes," she said as the ends of her lips turned up, and my head went back down.

"**C**lay, get up!" Bailey called hurriedly, scrambling her way from underneath the covers.

My eyes shot open, and in one fell swoop I was off the bed and on my feet. "What's wrong, Bailey? Are you okay?"

"I have to get home, I wasn't supposed to stay the night. I told Anne I would be home tonight. It's 4:30 in the morning!"

Shit. "Okay, come on," I said, gathering her stuff up and helping her to her minivan. Once we got there, I helped her in. "I'm sorry. I hope you don't get in trouble."

She smiled at me. "Even if I do, it will be worth it. I have to work today. A double too, ugh."

I leaned in, kissing her again. "I'll see you later tonight then. Be safe, text me when you get home, please."

"I will." She put the van in reverse and pulled away with a smile painted on her face.

An hour went by and I still hadn't heard from Bailey. I texted her, *"Hey, did you make it home?"* Another twenty minutes went by and still nothing. I was getting worried.

After another thirty minutes I sighed, sending her a final text before dozing off for much needed sleep. *"I enjoyed tonight. Hope you got home safe. Talk to you soon."*

I woke up later that morning around 10:30, rolling over to check my phone. The screen was bare with no messages. I was really worried now. What if something had happened to her on her way home? What if she regretted everything last night and was ignoring me?

A red circle with the number one prominently placed in the middle sat in the corner of one of my social media apps. Curious, I went into it to see one pending message. It was from LeeAnne Childe, it must have been Bailey's sister. Opening the message, it read *"Hey, this is Anne, Bailey's sister. She left her phone at your house, can you bring it by?"*

The message was a couple of hours old. My fears had been completely made up, figments of my imagination. The side effects of anxiety. I scavenged around my room, looking for her phone.

I couldn't get last night out of my mind. We had kissed for a good portion of the night. Yes, that was all we did. But it had been one of the best nights of my life. Being so close to her, holding her in my arms, feeling her hands on my body, tasting her on my lips, it was so perfect. She was still in my arms when we fell asleep. I remember hearing her breaths silently escaping her slightly opened mouth as she slept, the slow up and down movements of her chest as she breathed.

I finally found her phone underneath my bed. I quickly grabbed it and made my way to my car.

It took me about thirty minutes to get to her parent's driveway, where Bailey was staying for the summer. I brought my car to a stop and let it idle. I had never met any of her family, so it was a bit nerve wracking to even be here. I noticed the door of the house crack open and a taller female with red hair fashioned into a pixie haircut stepped out of the door and onto the deck. You could tell she and Bailey were sisters. Anne was taller, but they both had the same red hair and round faces accented by freckles.

She looked intimidating, as she stood there with her arms crossed, tapping her foot while I got out of the car. The nerves began creeping up on me, my stomach twisted in knots, and I began practicing what I was going to say over and over again in my head.

"So you're *the* Clay I have been hearing all about?" She asked as I walked up the steps. Even the tone in her voice was intimidating.

"I am." I extended my hand to her. "You must be Anne. I've heard a lot about you, I'm glad I finally get to meet you."

She looked me up and down, clicking her tongue against the roof of her mouth. "I've heard a lot about you, too. All of it good, but I'm going to warn you right now, that if you hurt my sister, I will hurt you. She deserves the best."

"I want you to hurt me if I ever hurt her. You're right. She deserves the best. She hasn't been given that in the past from what she's told me. She gives relationships her all, but they've always taken her for granted. I plan to give her all I have and then some, I plan to make her the happiest she has ever been, I plan on showing her what it's like to love and be loved."

I could see the anger slowly fading out of Anne's face as the words left my mouth. Her mouth relaxed, her eyes widened from their narrow state, and a smile was drawn across her face. The door opened behind her as a man her height walked out. He had short jet black hair, a face covered by an equally jet black beard, and he was slightly larger than me.

"Everything okay out here?" He asked as he walked out, his chest puffed out in an attempt to appear more intimidating. I had been more afraid of her than I was him.

Anne reached out and put her arm around the man, "Everything is okay. I think you're going to like him Chuck. This is Clay, Bailey's new boo. Clay, this is Chuck Carlson, my boyfriend."

I felt the red returning to my face. Bailey must have told her sister that I'd asked her out, which means she probably also told her she said yes. Maybe it wasn't a heat of the moment thing, maybe she really did want to be with me.

5

Our Best Friend

I walked into work, a red bowtie wrapped around the collar of my black button up shirt. When I was a server, I learned standing out from the crowd resulted in more tips. The more money, the better. It wasn't as if I made a lot of money to begin with. I had always been a bow tie extraordinaire, so I decided that would be my way to stand out. Then it just kind of stuck, people started to know me as the bowtie guy, so I kept the look when I became manager.

I had another reason for wanting to be dressed up today though. Bailey told me that if I was going to be with her, I would have to be approved by her best friend Mary, who was in town for a few days. Living up to the expectations and standards set forth by best friends was almost more terrifying than approval from the parents.

Best friends have more on the line than parents do in a sense--parents don't lose their place as parents. They'll always be in their child's life unless the child chooses otherwise. But best friends could lose their titles. If you've found love, you've also found your best friend in the whole world, which could make your previous best friends feel replaced or forgotten.

So it was understandable that they held the highest expectations for someone. I wanted to make a good impression. I wanted to show Mary she wouldn't lose Bailey. I wanted her to know that, if she would have me, she would be gaining another friend.

"Clay, Mrs. Bailey is here. Will you put the employee discount on her check? They've already ordered," Ma said, coming through the door to the dining room. "By the way, have you given any more thought to what I said a couple of weeks ago? About going out and trying to meet a nice girl not from this place?"

I reached back, rubbing the back of my neck. "Ma, I think I met someone. But I don't want to jinx it, so I'm keeping it quiet until things are a little more serious."

"You aren't even gonna tell your momma?" She laughed.

"In due time, Ma, in due time. You're going to love her though, I promise," I said as I left through the door she had just come out of, shouting "Coming out!"

As soon as I entered the dining room, I spotted Bailey across the restaurant. It was hard to miss her glowing red hair. It caught my attention first, but her personality was what won over my heart. She was sitting beside a shorter girl with shoulder length brown hair. Her makeup was put on a little more heavily than Bailey's ever was.

I made my way to the table, putting on my best manager face. "Good afternoon ladies, how're we doing this afternoon?"

Bailey blushed, pushing her hair out of her face, and tucking it behind her ear. Her friend, however, gave me the evilest eye I think I had ever seen. "We're doing good, Clay, thank you," Bailey chimed. "This is my best friend, Mary Kline."

I smiled, nodding in Mary's direction. "It's a pleasure to finally meet you. I've heard a lot of good things about you from Bailey."

She stared at me out of the corner of her eye, her nose snarled up. "You're Clay? Yeah, I've heard a lot about you too, and I know what it is you're doing here."

"Mary, keep it down," Bailey hushed her.

I chuckled, brushing the abruptness off. I understood where she was coming from, I really did. "Yes, that's me."

"Look," Mary started, turning her body towards me for the first time since I had arrived at the table. "I know what it is that you're doing, I know what the two of you have done, and I don't approve. I think you swooped in, tried to force her to break up with Blake, and then played the hero. I don't trust you. Until I get to know you, I won't trust you. Let's just hope I'm wrong, because this is my best friend, and I hate playing games when it comes to her."

I froze in my spot. I didn't expect winning her over to be easy, but I sure as hell didn't expect it to be this hard. "I get it, and I get your concern. In fact, I respect you even more for it. It means she has someone that loves her, someone that will do their best to protect her. And that is something that will help me sleep when y'all go back off to school. Knowing she has you makes me feel more comfortable. For that, I have to thank you." She shifted slightly in her seat, looking first to Bailey and then back at me. "Keep saying things like that, and I might end up liking you. Heavy emphasis on 'might', though," Mary said with what appeared to be a slight smile. She quickly wiped the smile from her face, probably hoping I wouldn't notice it.

As she finished, Ma came behind me with two plates of food. "Well ladies, you enjoy your food. Let Ma know if you need any- thing," I said, walking away. I quickly made my way to the back, worried what Ma may have overheard from our conversation. It was something I would have to face directly.

I sat at the computer in my office, checking numbers, when there was a soft knock at the door. I turned to see Ma waiting, her arms crossed as she looked at me. She heard.

"Come in," I said, waving her in.

"Clay." She started unstringing her serving apron and placed it on my desk. "Is that who you're seeing?"

I couldn't lie to her. "Yes, Ma. I'm sorry I didn't tell you sooner."

She smiled, leaning in to give me a hug. "I'm just happy you went outside of the restaurant to find someone. Even if they are a friend of someone who works here."

Did she think that I was talking about Mary? Should I go with it? Should I come clean? "Ma, will you close the door.".

She turned around, gently closing the door behind her. I shifted uncomfortably in my seat, sliding my leg underneath me on the chair. My foot shook rapidly, toe tapping the ground from my chair.

Ma turned back around, eyeing me suspiciously. "Who do you think it is that I'm seeing?" I asked, quirking an eyebrow.

"Miss Bailey's little friend. Isn't she the one?"

"Ma, it isn't Bailey's friend. It *is* Bailey. I know what you're going to say. I need to look outside of this place. But I'm telling you, there is something special about this girl. I see something different in her. I enjoy just being in her presence, talking to her. She really is amazing, I haven't felt like this about anyone. Not even Marissa, and you thought we were an amazing pair."

She took a deep breath, carefully contemplating her next words. She clicked her tongue and said, "Clay, if this is truly what makes you happy, then I'll take your word for it. I don't have a problem with Bailey. I just know your luck with the girls in here. Most of them don't want relationships. They just want hookups, and that isn't you anymore. I want you to be happy, and if this is it, I'll support it."

I let out a sigh of relief. I valued her opinion because she cared about me like she was my mom. In fact, she was a normal part of my 'meeting the parents' process. If she didn't like them, my real mom sure as hell wouldn't either.

I hadn't even been off work for five minutes before my phone dinged. *"Well, what did you think of Mary?"* the message from Bailey read.

I laughed to myself. I thought a lot of things about her, mainly good. *"She cares about you and I love that. She was brutally honest, and I can appreciate that too."*

"Believe it or not, you won her over."

"I did? It didn't seem like it lol." She sure had a strange way of showing me that she liked me.

"You didn't back down and cower when she tried to make you. She was testing you to see how much you actually cared for me. You showed her. And me."

"I meant what I said, Bailey. I feel better knowing you have someone like her up there. A best friend who is going to push you to be better, who is going to help you stay on track. I don't want her to feel like she's losing you as a friend, but that she's gaining me as a friend."

"You're something else Clay Dabrowski."

A few days later it was Bailey's turn to meet my best friend. Luke and I had been through a lot together. He took me under his wing when I was a lost eighteen-year-old kid trying to find my way in life. He may not have had the best influence on me in some regards, but he helped me to develop into who I was. He helped me through some dark times.

We decided to meet up at the pizzeria down the road from Luke's house. As Bailey and I pulled up, I saw his red lifted Chevy truck. I nodded at it with my head and turned to Bailey. "That's Luke's truck."

"Oh he's one of those lifted truck guys?" She chuckled.

I chuckled myself. Little did she know she would see a whole lot of that if she was hanging out with me. Personally, I wasn't into driving trucks, but a lot of my friends and family were into the jacked-up trucks. It was Myrtle Beach after all, and everyone down here drove big trucks. The kids from neighboring counties would even come to 'cruise' the strip in their jacked-up trucks.

I got out of the car, speed walking to the passenger door to open it for Bailey. She smiled a soft smile at me as she got out of the car, wrapping her arm around my waist as I closed the door. "Ready?" I asked.

She nodded and we walked into the pizzeria. As soon as we entered the restaurant, I could hear Luke yelling across the dining room. "Clay, buddy, over here!"

Bailey side-eyed me as we walked, whispering, "That's Luke?"

I couldn't help letting out a laugh. "Indeed it is." Luke was very outgoing, loud, some would even say obnoxious. I loved it about him because he didn't care what other people thought. He was always unapologetically him, and I respected and admired that.

We made our way to the table. I pulled Bailey's seat out and made my way into one beside her. Luke slapped the table, extending his hand to Bailey. "I'm Luke. I have heard so much about you!"

Bailey smiled, taking his large hand in her much smaller one. "Clay talks about you all the time!"

"All good I hope," Luke chuckled, turning to me. "How the hell are you man?"

I slid my hand over to Bailey's knee, her hand sneaking down and wrapping around mine. "Working, working, working. It's been so busy."

"I've been telling him he needs to find a different job. He isn't happy there anymore. You can tell when he's there. He has no life left in his eyes," Bailey said, squeezing my hand a little tighter and turning to look at me.

My gaze wandered away from hers, almost in shame. I knew she was right, I knew that place was draining me of my life, but I never thought I could achieve more. This was my ceiling.

"I've been trying to tell him that for months," Luke agreed as the waitress came to the table with a beer. She took our orders and left the table. Luke picked up the beer, downing it in almost a full gulp and continued. "Maybe you can talk some sense into him."

"Yeah, I think he's coming around to the idea." Bailey bit her lip, sensing the sadness in my eyes as they roamed back up to meet hers."This is my ceiling y'all. I know that. I've accepted that. It would be cool to get a job with my degree, but I have no experience. I spent all my college time working at The Door. Nobody is going to want to hire me."

"Clay." Luke glanced from to me to Bailey and then back to me. "You deserve more buddy. I know you. I know what you're capable of. I've seen what you can do when you put your mind to something. You're a hard worker, and any employer would be lucky to have you."

Bailey's eyebrows raised slightly as she listened to Luke. She squeezed my hand, causing me to look back at her. "He's right. He's known you longer than me, so if you don't believe me, believe him."

I chewed on my lip, mulling over both Luke and Bailey's words. How could they both have the same opinion and be wrong? Was I just being my own worst enemy? Or were they just being good friends? "Yeah, maybe." I shifted uncomfortably in my seat, letting go of Bailey's hand and turning my attention to the hot and bubbly cheese and pepperoni pizza that was being dropped off at the table.

I had been quiet the rest of the meal, letting Luke and Bailey talk and get to know one another. I was stuck in my own mind the entire time, wondering if I could be more. The back and forth in my mind was excruciating,

"You are more than that place."

"No you aren't, you have no experience."

"So? I have managerial experience now. I can relate job duties to jobs in my field."

"Good luck with that. You have ZERO experience in the field."

"But I can't get experience if I don't try to get a job in that field."

"You should have got experience while you were in college. Taken some internships."

"I had to work so I could pay my way through school, afford to live."

"So you valued money over experience?"

"Well when you put it that way--"

"Exactly. You screwed up your entire life. What are you going to do if you start applying to hundreds of jobs and don't get a call back?"

"But what if I do get a call back?"

"Can you handle hundreds of rejections before getting a call-back?"

"No. I have a job, no sense in looking elsewhere."

As Bailey and I said our goodbyes to Luke and we got back into my car, I brought the car to life. The roar of the engine drowned out my thoughts. I closed my eyes and took a deep breath.

"What's wrong, Clay?" Bailey asked, taking my hand in hers and gently running her fingers up and down my arm.

"Nothing, I'm just tired." It wasn't far from the truth, I WAS tired. But she didn't need to know about the twenty-minute conversation I'd had in my head while we'd been eating. "What did you think about Luke?"

"He's a little on the crazy side, isn't he?"

I laughed, finally turning my eyes to her. "He is. But he is who he is, and he takes pride in that. I hope to get to his level one day."

"You don't think a lot of yourself, do you?"

I bit my lip, debating on what to say next. "There's not much about me to feel good about." I sighed, staring into her eyes. She stared back at me, our gazes locked. It was as if we were looking into one another's soul.

"Clay, you are special. I wish I could get you to see that. But I am glad you'll have Luke when I'm away for school. He cares about you, a lot. And while he may be on the wild side, I think he does you a lot of good. He *is* your biggest supporter right now. I'm thankful that you have him."

"Yeah," I started, my eyes never leaving hers. "Me too."

A First for Everything

I slipped into my nicest pair of dark blue, slim fit jeans. Bailey and I were going on our first date that wasn't just dinner. I don't know why I was so nervous, I just wanted to make sure she had a good time, and I didn't want her to regret being with me. The last few weeks had been the happiest I had ever been in my life since the night I'd gained the courage to ask her to be mine. I was sure she only said yes in the heat of the moment, but it turned out she really did mean it.

I grabbed a white shirt from my closet, sliding it over my head. I went into the bathroom, looking at myself in the mirror. My hair slicked to the side, my beard combed out down my chin, I felt like I actually looked decent for once.

"You got this," I said to myself in the mirror. "She likes you. She likes you. Have some faith, some confidence. Show her how much you like her. Make her happy."

"What the hell are you doing in there?" Brian called from the living room of our apartment. Instant embarrassment flooded me.

"Getting ready for a date man," I called back after an awkward silence.

"Soooo," he started, pausing dramatically. "You're talking to yourself? What? Are you your own hype man now?"

I walked to the living room, plopping down on the couch beside Brian while the tv played in the background. "You're damn right I am. If you can't love yourself, how can you expect to love anyone else?"

"You're in love already?"

"No, I'm just saying. If I want to find love, I have to love myself first."

"Clay, how would you feel about meeting my parents?" Bailey asked from the passenger seat of the Challenger. She shifted her body, folding one leg up on the seat, and propped her hands up on the center console.

I took a big gulp. I had won over her best friend, so the parents were the next step. I was usually good with parents--they loved me. But some sinking feeling kept telling me they would hate me.

"Sure," I finally mustered.

She took my free hand in hers, lightly rubbing my knuckles with her fingers. It was the little touches like that which sent my body into a frizzy. I loved her touch and the way it made me feel.

"Are you sure?" Her tone filled with concern as she cocked her head to the side.

I shifted my hand, moving it over top of hers. I squeezed her hand just tightly enough to make sure we were as close as possible without hurting her. "I want to meet everyone you love, everyone who is important to you. Because one day, I want them to be important to me too. I want them to love me like they love you and I want to love them like you love them."

She smiled her beautiful smile, fluttering her eyelashes in my direction. "Clay, why are you so damn perfect?"

I chuckled. I had been called a lot of things, perfect was not among those. "Bailey, I'm only perfect for the most perfect girl. Look at the way our hands fit together." I nodded down at our hands perfectly complementing one another, our fingers filling in the spaces between one another's knuckles like they were meant to be there.

She looked down at our hands and then back up at me, a smile painted across her face. She was the most beautiful person I had ever met. Her smile radiated happiness and I couldn't help but be in a good mood when she was smiling. Her eyes, though, were what gave me chills the most. I hadn't told her a lot about my past aside from the bit at dinner the first night we hung out. Yet, every time she looked into my eyes, I felt like she knew, she understood, and she was telling me it was okay.

We pulled into the parking lot of my favorite arcade in town. I hadn't told her where we were going; I just wanted to surprise her. The arcade was complete with go-karts, games, mini golf, and laser tag. We had a lot to choose from, and I thought we would have a lot of fun.

"You know," Bailey started, opening the door of the car and crawling out. "I've never been here."

"Really?" I was genuinely shocked. "This is where I had most of my birthday parties as a kid. I always loved playing laser tag and riding the go-karts, playing all the games and getting enough tickets to get candy from the prize counter. They even had some really good pizza in the cafe."

She laughed a little as I reminisced. "What do you have planned for us to do first?"

I took her by the hand, leading her through the doors and to the arcade counter.

"Two go-kart tickets and two mini golf tickets, please," I said to the clerk. My hand was still wrapped tightly around Bailey's. I embraced the warmth she was giving off in the cold building.

I took the tickets and led her out the double doors to the go-kart track. I stopped her before we got in line, wrapping my arm around her waist, and pulling her in for a kiss. Her lips brushed mine, filling in the gap in my mouth. It was perfect. She was perfect. I rested my head on hers with my eyes closed, a smile forming across my lips. My heart raced, racing from the exhilaration.

We made our way to the front of the line, hand-in-hand. I looked over to her, a smile creeping up on my face mischievously. "Are you ready?".

"No holding back." She playfully elbowed my side.

"No holding back," I repeated as we were let into the go-kart area.

We found our way to the two go-karts in the head of the line, her in the first and me in the second. She looked back at me with her hair tucked into her white helmet. Her eyes shone with joy as the lights in front of us went from red to yellow to green. She took off as soon as the light hit green, and I took off after her.

Around each curve we went, her keeping a steady lead on me for most of the track. As we got to one of the last curves, she slowed down. I sped up a little bit, slightly bumping into the back of her go-kart. I heard her giggles over the buzz of the go-kart's engine.

I slid my go-kart to the right, sneaking up beside her. I looked over at her. She wore the biggest smile I had ever seen on her. I smiled back, turning my go-kart into hers, slightly bumping her again. More laughter erupted from both of us as she sped up, trying to get out of reach.

We pulled back into the go-kart lanes, unstrapping our seatbelts, and hopping out. Bailey ran up to me, nearly jumping into my arms. I wrapped my arms around her waist, pulling her in. She rested her head against my chest as she squeezed me.

"That was so fun!" She looked up at me.

I smiled, taking her hand in mine again and began leading her to the mini golf course. "Are you any good?" I asked as we grabbed our golf clubs from the shack at the mini golf course.

"I'm not too shabby," she said, grabbing a yellow handled club.

"Good, because I am very shabby." I laughed, grabbing a blue handled club.

"Is there more about you I don't know yet?" She joked, wiggling her eyebrows at me. Well, she thought she was joking anyways.

"Oh there are quite a few things you don't know about me. As I'm sure there is a lot about you that I don't know." When we got to the first hole, I turned to her and took her hands, continuing, "But that's the exciting part about dating. We get to know one another on a deeper, more intimate level. We get to learn each other's little quirks and secrets and learn to love them."

She blushed, looking down at my feet. "Hey, those are your work shoes! You weren't kidding about wearing those everywhere."

I shrugged, setting my ball down. "I told you they were comfortable." I readied myself, doing my best golf impression. I wiggled my butt a couple of times in Bailey's direction and turned around to wink at her. I tapped the ball, watching it roll in a straight line, up a hill, and then back down the side of the hill, falling right into the hole. I looked over at her and winked. "Did I say I was shabby? Whoops."

"I'm impressed, but you're going to have to make more than just one to qualify as not too shabby sir." Bailey smiled, laying her ball down next. She planted her feet, mocking my butt wiggle. Her butt was perfect though, round and perky. I bit my lip, holding back my urges to rush her and kiss her again and again, grabbing her butt and feeling it in between my fingers. She tapped the ball, but she rounded the hill and dropped it into the hole. "Two can play that game," she said, poking my stomach with the end of her club.

I grabbed her wrist, spinning her into me. I draped my arms over her shoulders, connecting behind her neck. I leaned in, kissing her deeply. She let out a quiet moan into my mouth as we continued to kiss. I worked my hands down to her butt, feeling it with my hand. I grabbed and squeezed, causing her to let out a yelp.

"Come on, Tiger Woods, we're holding up the game," she giggled, nodding at the people waiting in line behind us.

I pulled into the parking spot beside Bailey's van, bringing the car to a stop. I looked at her, sitting in all her beauty in my passenger seat. Tonight had been perfect, the most perfect "first date". The laughs we shared, the memories we were building--it was all worth everything. I looked over at her, the side of her face resting against the seat while she faced me.

"What's on your mind, beautiful?" I asked her, leaning in and placing a small kiss on her cheek.

"You." She smiled, moving her hand to mine, entwining our fingers.

"Me?" I asked, pointing at myself. "What did I do?"

"How were you single? You're perfect on so many levels, you have a way with your words, and you have such a big heart. So how were you single?"

"I have a long, complicated past, Bailey. One I want to tell you all about eventually, but for now I will tell you this." I brushed her cheek with the side of my finger and looked into her eyes. I wanted her to see within me, to understand more, to be a part of me. "The last long-term relationship I had was in high school. We were together for three years. I was, I thought, in love. I looked at rings for when we graduated. But my senior year it all collapsed on itself."

She raised an eyebrow, leaning her head off the seat, cocking it slightly to the side. "What does that mean?"

I sighed, not wanting to relive the memories of my last serious relationship but knowing I had to. "Rumors had always flown around about her cheating on me. And despite insurmountable evidence, messages, pictures, even seeing with my own eyes, I brushed them off. I thought I was the love of her life and she would always be mine and I would always be hers. I thought I would always be the one she came to at the end of the day and I was okay with that. Things got rocky towards the end. She started cheating on me more. She ignored me for days on end, told people we had broken up when we hadn't, and I finally got tired of it.

"I stood up for myself, finally. I broke things off with her. When I did, I had to know the truth. So I asked her how many people she actually cheated on me with. Twenty-four people. Not times, people. Multiple times with most of them, either flirting or more. I was devastated. I haven't trusted anyone since. Most of the time, my trust issues get in the way of my relationships and I break them off before I can get hurt," I finally finished, looking down at our hands.

Her grip on my hand tightened. I looked back up and into her eyes. I saw pain, but it wasn't her pain. It was mine; she hurt for me, for my past. Then it shifted to anger, anger that anyone would do that to me. "Why would she do that? Why would anyone do that?"

I shrugged my shoulders, at a loss for words.

"Clay." She reached up and tilted my chin. "Don't give up on me."

I looked into her eyes again. She was afraid that I would end up leaving her because of my past, like I had left all the others. I had never seen this look of wanting to stay with me, but it made my stomach turn somersaults.

"I know this is asking a lot, but I need you to try and trust me. Don't give up on me. Don't give up on us. Whatever we may face, whatever issues we may have, we can work through them together. Just have faith, please."

I didn't know what to say. No girl had ever wanted this, had ever tried to get me to stay before I even tried to leave. She cared about me, a lot. Something about this relationship was different, I knew that from the first time I met her, but this just affirmed everything. "I will do my best, Bailey, that I can promise you. And promises are something sacred to me, I don't use them unless they're true. I feel like I need to have something that makes other people confident they can trust me."

She smiled, leaning over and hugging me around the neck. "I love you." She immediately let go of my neck. "I'm sorry, I shouldn't have said that," she said as she continued to gather her things. Before I could even respond, she was standing outside of the car.

"I'll text you when I get home."

I woke up the next morning, my mind still racing about what had happened yesterday. She'd told me she loved me, and while we had only been together for a matter of weeks, something about her words seemed genuine. Something about the look in her eyes, the innocence in her tone, the way she wanted me to not give up on her, all made it seem so pure.

What worried me, though, was the fact that she'd freaked out when she'd said it. She'd texted me when she got home and immediately said she was going to bed. Maybe she didn't mean it and had only said it in the heat of the moment. She could have freaked herself out by saying it, not expecting it to come in just a few weeks. Maybe she'd just said it to make me feel better. Whatever the reason, I had to find out.

When the words had left her mouth and floated gently into my ears like a feather, something inside of me lit up. A new flame burned within me, lighting my soul on fire again. I hadn't heard those words since I'd broken up with Ashley, but something about those three simple words escaping her mouth, in her voice, made me want more.

I think I loved her, too. Sure, it was quick. But when I first met her, I thought I was going to marry her. Something about her was different, and maybe this was it.

I got dressed and headed down the road to get lunch. I sat in a booth in the corner of a taco joint, staring at the phone in my hand while the food sitting on the black cafeteria style tray underneath my hands got cold. My nerves were curving my appetite as I tried to figure out what to text Bailey.

"Last night when you said you loved me, did you mean it?" Was what I finally decided on. But as soon as I hit send, I had anxiety again. Was that too abrupt? Should I have started off with a simple 'Hey'?

I sat there eating my food, my phone laying on the table beside me with the message arrived. Finally typing bubbles came up on the screen. Then disappeared. Then reappeared.

"I didn't mean to say it. But I think I do."

"I think I love you too Bailey."

My heart beat within my chest. Love was a strong word; it was a strong feeling. Last time I was in love, I'd gotten hurt. I'd gotten hurt and had never thought I would come back from it. Bailey helped me see the light, see that I could be in love again.

But I was still hesitant. I couldn't help it. My walls were up, and while I felt like I was falling in love, I knew I had to protect myself. Love was sneaking up on me again, and I was terrified.

Meet the Parents

The day came when it was time to meet the parents. We were meeting her parents for breakfast and mine for dinner. I was nervous to say the least. But in the same sense, I was excited. This would be a big step for us, for me. It had been so long since I had met the parents, I was afraid of screwing it up.

My mom was cautious about the girls I'd brought home--her standards were much higher than mine. She still viewed me as her little boy and would always do so. She believed I only deserved the best. She had seen me beat down in the past, and I knew how much it hurt her to see me used and abused.

I was just going to be unequivocally me. Their daughter loved me for who was, so they should too. Family had always been a big thing for me. I valued and treasured those who were there for me, my true family.

Growing up with divorced parents was hard, but having family on one side who loved me and cherished me helped me through the dark times. I wanted to be part of their family one day because of the way Bailey talked about them.

Bailey had stayed at my apartment the night before--something she was starting to do a little more now that she was allowed. It was nice to have her laying in my arms, her head against my chest, my lips pressed against the top of her head. I gently shook her and whispered, "Time to get up baby."

She shifted her body slightly, nuzzling my chest. "Can't we just lay here for another five minutes?"

"I wish we could," I started. "But we have to meet your parents in an hour."

She let out a groan and rolled out of the bed. "Fine. But we're coming back here to lay down after breakfast."

"Deal," I laughed. We got along so well, and we were alike in more ways than we had realized. She was becoming my best friend more and more every day. "Now go get dressed so we can go."

She looked up at me, biting her lip softly. That look in her eyes always caused my heart to skip a beat. I wanted to see that look for the rest of my life. She wrapped her arms around my shoulder, planting a kiss on my cheek. "I'll be right back, handsome."

As we pulled into the parking lot of the breakfast place, Bailey looked over at me. "Are you nervous?"

My chuckle practically answered for me. "A little bit. I really want them to like me. I know how much their opinion means to you."

I saw out of the corner of my eye that she smiled. She hopped out of the car as I cut off the engine. I followed her out and into the restaurant, where her parents waited for us.

We walked in and glanced around at the busy restaurant. Bailey scanned the sea of heads until she came across her parents. She pointed them out to me and waved her hand. She took my hand and led me to their table.

"Mom, Dad this is Clay. Clay, these are my parents, Maye and Kenny Frey." We slid into the booth with them.

I extended my hand to Maye first. "It's a pleasure to meet you both," I said with a cheesy smile on my face. She was about the same size as Bailey. They really could have been mistaken for sisters. The only difference was Maye's shoulder length hair was a deep black. But her face was full of freckles just like Bailey, they had the same loving eyes, and shared a nose.

"Clay, it's good to meet you sweetie," she said with a smile, reaching out and gently taking my hand. "We've heard so many good things about you."

"Thank you, ma'am. I have heard so many good things about you as well," I said, releasing her hand and extending it to Kenney. "Thank you for having breakfast with me this morning."

"It's no problem," Kenney said as he gripped my hand tightly. He squeezed a little harder than he probably normally did, trying to assert his dominance as the father. He was about my height, slightly taller than his wife. His long brown hair was slicked back, and he sported a beard. He was stone faced, his expression un-readable.

The waitress came and took our orders, collecting the menus before returning to the kitchen. Kenney directed his attention to me next. "So Bailey tells us you're the manager at The Door?"

"Yes sir. I've been there for about three years. I just graduated with my communications degree though, and after a lot of conversations with Bailey, I think I'm going to start looking for a job in my field."

"That's good. Bailey is going to always push you to be better, and you can't help but to love her for it. Because she's Bailey," Maye laughed.

"So your last name, where is it from?" Kenney asked.

"Poland," I said proudly. I loved my heritage; it was something in which I took a lot of pride. I had done a lot of research into my family history, and it was really cool to see the connections. "Hey, want to hear a joke?"

Everyone looked around at one another and smiled. Kenney spoke up first. "Tell us what you've got."

"Alright, so there was this comedian ventriloquist who was doing a show. He began telling a blonde joke and a young lady in the crowd shoots up. She points at the stage and says 'Hey, what gives you the right to make fun of someone just for their hair color?'

"The man stumbles over his words, trying to apologize. She looks at him and says 'Stay out of this! This is between me and the dummy!'"

The table erupted in laughter. Bailey looked over at me, taking my hand in hers, and squeezing slightly. We smiled at one another. I felt like I was going to fit right in.

By the end of the meal, we were all laughing at jokes told around the table. We had really clicked, and my anxiety eased a little. When the waitress came to the table, she asked about checks.

"It can all be on one," I said. I wanted to show them respect and appreciation for hearing me out, talking and listening to me. For giving me a chance.

"Oh sweetie," Maye said. "You don't have to do that!"

My smile was big and genuine. "Ma'am, it would be my pleasure. It's my thank you for coming."

After I paid, we all went to our cars where we stood chatting for a while "I wasn't sure about you at first," Kenney admitted. "The way things happened so quickly after Blake, it made me a little nervous. I felt like you swooped in."

The anxiety returned. I knew that would be one of the things her parents may hold against me, and sure enough I had been right. "I understand, sir. I do. But I want you to know I really care about your daughter. I would do anything for her, and I would do anything for y'all as well."

"I see that now. You seem like a really good guy," he said, still stone faced.

"I think you're good for our daughter," Maye spoke up. "You'll take care of her, and I think you two will encourage one another. You two make a power couple."

That was probably one of the best things I could have heard at that moment. It made me so happy to know they both thought so highly of me, and of us as a couple. We said our goodbyes. Bailey and I walked back to my car.

"I think that went well," I said, opening her door for her.

"That went better than I could have expected. They loved you Clay. They hardly like anybody like that." Bailey turned and leaned into me.

I wrapped my arms around her, pulling her in. I lifted her chin up and pressed my lips on hers, brushing the tip of my nose against hers. "I love you," I murmured against her open lips.

"I love you, too," she said into my mouth as she kissed me again.

I woke up a few hours later, still holding Bailey in my arms. Her chest raised and lowered slowly as she breathed, air quietly escaping the space between her lips. I almost didn't want to wake her up for the second time today; she seemed so peaceful. I reached up, gently stroking her head, my hands tracing her hair.

She stirred a bit, rolling over to face me. Her eyes slowly fluttered open, blinking a few times quickly. Her eyes met mine. A smile crept across her face. "Well that was nice," she sighed.

I picked up my phone, checking the time. "We've got about thirty minutes before we need to leave." I rolled out of bed and extended my hand to her to help her off the bed.

She took my hand, using it as support. I pulled her into my chest, wrapping my arms around her and kissing the top of her head gently. "I'm so excited for you to meet my family."

She looked up, her arms draped across my shoulders. "I'm excited to meet the people who helped make you who you are," she said. "Plus all the things you've told me about your mom is exciting."

I smiled. It was a good feeling to have her want to meet my family, to have her desire to fit in and join our family. I had a real feeling my mom would love her, and she would love my mom. After the disaster with my high school sweetheart, my mom had become even less trusting of the girls I brought home.

We finished getting ready for dinner, she wanted to 'look her best' for meeting my mom, her words not mine. I thought she looked gorgeous no matter what and all the time, but I guess she didn't see it in her own eyes.

After showers, we got dressed and made our way out to my car. "So you really think your parents like me?" I asked Bailey from the driver's seat.

"Absolutely. Mom even texted me shortly after we left talking about how much she liked you. She even said daddy did too." She reached over and took my free hand as I drove.

"Really?" I smiled at the thought. "I really liked both of your parents. I can see us getting along really well."

"You were amazing, Clay." she gently rubbed my hand in hers.

"I do have a question that has been sitting on my mind," I confessed to her.

She raised an eyebrow and scrunched her nose as she turned to look at me. "Go on..."

"Why do your parents have a different last name than you?"

She chuckled a little before answering. "Kenney is my stepdad. He might as well be my dad, though. I haven't talked to my real dad in years, and honestly I have no desire to talk to him."

"My parents aren't together either. My stepdad is about like yours it sounds like. I call him my dad. And he is in every sense of the word," I told her. "My dad and I don't exactly have the best relationship, we've never really gotten along."

"My real dad left shortly after I was born. He helped raise my brother and sister, but he really never had anything to do with me," she started, her tone turning sourer. "Out of the three of us, it was never me that he would come and get to spend the weekend. Honestly, though, I'm glad it worked out that way because I got daddy out of it."

I gripped her hand tightly, squeezing it so she knew I was there for her, wanting to comfort her, ease her pain. We pulled onto the dirt road that led to my mom's house. It was my childhood home, a grey two-story brick house. It had been my great grandparent's house originally, passed down to my mom after they'd passed away. I loved it, The wide window in the front that faced the woods, where we used to sit and play as kids, watching for animals scurrying about.

We came to a stop, and I looked over at Bailey, nervousness setting in her expression. "You ready?"

She took a deep breath, inhaling and exhaling sharply. Looking over at me, she forced a smile. "As I'll ever be."

We made our way into the house, passing through the screen door to be greeted by the barks of my mom's pug, Pops. I crouched down on my knees as the grey-haired pug ran up and jumped into my lap, knocking me onto the ground. "Hey buddy!" I said in between licks. I reached down and rubbed both of his ears with the palm of my hand, his tongue falling out the side of his mouth and his eyes shut.

Bailey knelt beside me, rubbing the top of Pops' head. He opened his eyes, darting them over at her. He pulled away cautiously, sniffing at her hands. He walked around her, sniffing. Finally, he jumped up on her, his paws pressed against her shoulders, and began licking her face.

Mom came to the entryway where we were standing, still dressed in her grey t-shirt and sweatpants. Her long blonde hair hung down her back, her eyes matched mine almost perfectly. Pops jumped off Bailey and went to stand in between mom's legs. "Hey, Mom," I said as I stood. "This is Bailey. Bailey, this is my mom, Susan Crawford."

Bailey stood beside me, her beautiful smile sprawled across her lips, and extended her hand. "It is such a pleasure to meet you Mrs. Crawford, I have heard so much about you."

Mom reached out, taking her hand. She was smiling, which hardly ever happened when she met one of the girls, I brought home. It was normally a simple tolerating smile with the others, but instantly she was amazed by Bailey. "Please," she started. "Call me Susan. Clay has told me so much about you, so many good things. The pleasure, sweetie, is all mine."

We went into the living room, taking a seat on the loveseat while Mom sat with her legs thrown up on the couch. "Where's Matt?" I cracked open a can of Pepsi from Mom's fridge.

"He'll be in shortly. He's working on his truck," Mom started, turning back to face Bailey. "I just love your hair."

Bailey playfully tossed the curls of her blazing red hair to the side and said, "Thank you so much!"

"It was what first caught my attention," I said, leaning into her. "And the rest will be history one day."

Mom looked over at Bailey and me, as we stared into one another's eyes. Out of the corner of my eye I saw the biggest smile I had ever seen on Mom's face. It made me happy to see that look. I knew she wanted to see me happy, and her happiness made mine feel real. It didn't feel like I was being a hopeless romantic anymore, I felt like I was truly in love.

Pops started barking again, sliding across the hardwood floors as he struggled to get a grip, making his way to the backdoor. We heard the door open, and Matt's voice followed as he greeted Pops. He walked into the living room and sat down beside Mom. He was a bit taller than me, but we were about the same size. Sideburns led from the side of his shaggy dirty blonde hair, down to his goatee that rounded off his face.

"Honey," Mom started, turning towards Matt. "This is Bailey, Clay's girlfriend. Bailey, this is my husband Matt."

Matt nodded in her direction with a smile. It was rare to see a smile on his face. He was typically reserved and hid his emotions. Seeing him smile at Bailey further reassured me that she was right for me. "It's a pleasure to meet you, sir," Bailey said.

Matt chuckled. "Oh, you can call me Matt. Looks like you're going to be part of this family."

Bailey's face lit up with happiness, her eyes glowing. She was so happy to hear him say that she would be part of the family, and that excitement was part of the reason I was falling so in love with her. She placed the same value and importance on family I did.

"So Bailey, Clay says you're going to school at Converse College?" Mom asked.

"Yes, ma'am." Bailey's face was still lit with a smile. She radiated beauty. "I'll be a sophomore this upcoming year."

"What're you going to school for?" Matt chimed in.

"I'm going for a degree in health and nutrition, but I'm minoring in coaching. I play soccer for Converse now, and I'm hoping to be able to coach some after I graduate," Bailey started. "I was going to do a minor in business, but accounting was kicking my butt. I'm not very good at math."

"Oh Clay is great at math!" Mom cheered, clapping her hands. "Maybe you could change your minor back to business and do coaching as your major." I loved the fact that Mom already supported her in all the same ways I was and trying to encourage her to do better just like she did with me and my brother Josh. She treated Bailey like she was her own daughter already.

We heard the door open again and Pops took off towards the door. This time it was Josh. He was about the same height as Matt, his short hair the same color as mine. He was the athletic type, playing baseball, basketball, and football for his high school.

"What's up, Josh?" I said from the couch as he walked in.

Josh turned towards me, his eyes moving from me to Bailey and back to me. He wiggled his eyebrows. "Is this one of your girlfriends you've been telling me about?"

"Josh!" Mom had a look of anger in her eyes as she stared him down for his comment. "You'll have to ignore him," Mom said to Bailey, waving my brother off.

I chuckled. "Bailey, this is my brother Josh. He *thinks* he's funny."

"I'm just kidding, Bailey," Josh laughed. I couldn't tell if he was saying that on his own or if it was because of the look Mom gave him. You know *that look* moms give you. "It's nice to finally meet you. In all seriousness, Clay talks about you all the time. More than any girl he's dated really."

I nodded. He wasn't wrong, I talked about Bailey a lot. That's just because she was that amazing to me. Everything she did was great, anything she put her mind to she excelled at.

After about an hour of eating dinner, chatting, and laughing with my family, we decided to go visit my grandparents. They lived right beside my mom in a small red brick house. They had built that house in the 60's and had lived there ever since.

My grandparents were just as important to me as my parents. They helped Mom raise me. My childhood had been equally spent with them as much as with Mom. Matt was like my dad in the sense of being the one that came into my life, but I truly considered my grandpa my *dad.* He had always been there for my entire life. He was my father figure.

When we walked over, we spotted my grandma and grandpa sitting outside on their covered, screened in, wrap around porch. They both loved sitting out there, even on the hot summer days because they had ceiling fans out there. They loved their porch.

"Hey Ma, hey Pa," I said with a big smile. I loved seeing them. "This is my girlfriend, Bailey. Bailey, this is my grandma Susan and grandpa Gib."

"She's a cute one, Clay. You did good boy," Pa chuckled. He and I were very similar in size and looks. His grayed hair, though, was buzzed with a flat top. His skin was bronzed from years of running his own construction company. His father before him had started it and now Matt ran it.

"Oh behave," Ma laughed, swatting at him playfully. Her short gray hair poofed up in such a cute way, it made her tiny stature complete. Even in their old age, they still played and loved each other like the day they met. "Honey, it is so nice to meet you. Clay has told us so much about you."

Bailey smiled wide, her white teeth shining. "I'm so glad I get to meet you! I know how important you've both been to Clay's life. He turned out amazing." She leaned into me as I wrapped my arm around her.

"Would you like a glass of sweet tea honey?" Ma really wasn't asking. She was going to serve her sweet tea. She was so proud of her sweet tea. Before Bailey could answer she was pouring tea from the pitcher sitting beside her into an empty mason jar.

Bailey took it, sipping the tea. Her eyes widened and her eyebrows shot up. "That's delicious!"

Pa laughed. "You're gonna fit in just fine, honey." And he was right. She was natural with my family. She really could be one of us.

Later that night, after Bailey had gone home and I had gone back to my apartment, I sat in my bed that was folded into a couch. I was so curious to know what Mom thought. It meant a lot for me to get her opinion, she was normally always spot on with these things.

So I texted Mom. *"What did you think about Bailey?"*

Almost immediately, she texted me back. *"She's a keeper, Clay."*

"I know Mom. I've never felt this way before."

"I have a feeling she's going to be part of our family one day."

<h1 style="text-align:center">Camping Trip</h1>

A knock and wiggle of the doorknob came at the door of my apartment. I hopped off the couch and went to the door. Through the peephole I saw Luke, well his bushy brown beard. I opened the door, letting him in.

"What's going on, Luke?" I asked as he walked to the fridge and grabbed a beer for both of us.

"This weekend we're going camping. Bring Bailey," Luke said with a large smile, excitement building in his tone. Luke was the first one I had told about Bailey and me, after all he was my best friend.

"Man I highly doubt her parents are going to let her go," I said, leaning up against the counter.

Luke plopped down on a bar stool. He put the bottle to his mouth, biting the top off with his teeth. "Her parents? Isn't she like 19?"

"Yeah, but she lives with her parents when she's not four hours away at school, so she kinda has to follow their rules," I snapped back. Luke wasn't big on the rules. I got it. I wasn't huge on them anymore either, but I still would have respected my parents' decision if I were living under their roof.

"Her parents have been letting her stay with me every now and again, but a whole weekend out of town is going to be hard to swing," I finished.

"Well at least ask her man. I would love for y'all to come with Ally and me," he pleaded. "Her parents have a RV they're going to let us use. It's gonna be so fun man. It's getting cool outside, and the leaves are starting to change colors. We'll sit around the fire and drink some beer, roast weenies, and make s'mores."

"I'll ask. Either way, I'll go with y'all. I need a vacation anyway." I tipped the bottle to my lips, letting the cold beer flow down my throat. I needed a vacation, a getaway from life. I was working so much I hadn't been taking time for myself.

Luke slapped me on the back, standing up. "You do man. You need to relax," he said, walking to the kitchen and setting the bottle down on the counter and heading to the door. He paused when he grabbed the doorknob. "Let me know what she says," he called over his shoulder as he left the apartment.

The next day, I slid a white shirt over my body, the cloth clinging to my bare skin as I closed the dresser drawer behind me. I looked to Bailey, laying in my bed staring at me as I got ready for work. "Hey," I called out, pulling a bowtie off the rack in my closet. "Have you ever been camping?"

"Like in the woods?" Bailey asked back, looking at me with a raised eyebrow, curiosity filling her eyes.

"Yes, like in the woods," I chuckled. "Luke wants to go camping this weekend. I know it's short notice..."

"Yes, I'll go." She clapped, sitting up cross legged on the bed. "I'll have to tell my parents I'm going to stay with Mary for the weekend though, so we have to be extra careful."

I turned around, stuffing my shirt into the waist of my slacks. I grabbed a black button up, slipping my arm through the holes. "And you think she'll go for that?"

"The more I talk to her about you, the more she loves you." She smiled, taking my hands in hers, looking up into my eyes. "And the more I love you, Clay Dabrowski."

I leaned down, planting a kiss firmly on her forehead. She really was turning out to be my dream girl. "I've got to head to work baby, I'll text you when I get there. Lock the door on your way out please." I said as I left the apartment.

I pulled into Luke's driveway after work. I went to his house after work quite frequently, pretty much any day I wasn't with Bailey. Luke was like a brother to me, even though we weren't blood.

His house was an old farm style house, with a wraparound porch that had ceiling fans all throughout. Rocking chairs and tiny tables lined the porch. The grey siding was accented by the white trim and gutters running along the roof.

It was late, but Luke was always up late. As I turned my car off, the porch light of Luke's house lit up bright. Getting out of the car, I heard Luke walk out the front door followed by the pitter patter of dog paws. "Hey buddy!" He called out, sitting on a chair in front of the house. His golden retriever Lilith ran off the porch, jumping up on me. I rubbed the top of her head.

I walked up to the chair next to him and sat down, pulling a cigarette out of my pocket. Luke already had a beer opened for me on the table and one raised to his lips. "So Bailey is good to go for this weekend," I said, lighting the cigarette in between my lips.

"Hell yeah," he shouted, punching his fist in the air. "Man, this is going to be a good time, I'm telling you."

I chuckled, the ember at the end of my cigarette shining brighter with each inhale of smoke. "Man, I'm excited. I'm really excited to be able to spend more time with Bailey though. She's turning into everything I ever wanted in a girl."

"That serious, huh?" He asked, a look of curiosity growing on his face as he cocked his head to the side.

"I'm telling you, this is the girl." I replied.

"You really think this is the girl?"

"I do," I said without hesitation. I knew it was fact, it had to be. Something about her, about the way her voice rang in my ears and soothed me, the way her smile lightened my mood, it just made sense. We had made sense from the day I met her, and the affirmation only grew stronger with each passing day.

"I've noticed a difference in you, you're happier."

"I feel happier. I'm even looking for other jobs, she's encouraged me to start bettering myself and to use my degree. To get out of The Door"

"Dude, I've been telling you you're too good for The Door. They're using you, from restaurant to restaurant, burning you out, and not paying you what they're paying the other managers," he said as he rolled his eyes and sipped his beer.

He was right. He had been telling me that for a while. The truth was, though, I never felt like I was better than that. I thought that was what I deserved. But Bailey had made me see otherwise, she helped me realize my potential, helped me to see my own worth. She boosted my confidence.

"I know, but she makes me feel it," I started, finishing off my beer. "No offense, but there's something in her that inspires me. To be better."

Bailey and I sat in the back of the RV while Luke drove, Ally at his side in the passenger seat. Bailey had her hair tied back in a ponytail like a fiery lion's mane lining her back. Her purple tank top fit her curves perfectly, accenting them as it ran down her body. She was as beautiful as ever.

I leaned over and whispered, "Are you excited?

She looked at me, gripping my hands tightly in hers. "I'm always excited to be spending time with you, Clay. Being around you has made me the happiest I have been in a long time, maybe even ever. I love your family too. Your mom was so sweet."

Every time I heard her voice, she stole my heart a little more. Like a lullaby to calm a restless baby, her voice always calmed my restless mind. My restless mind, however, would not rest for long. All I could think about was the deepest, darkest secret I held. I hadn't told very many people, not even Bailey yet. I knew I needed to, and I planned to do it while we were on the camping trip. Just not now.

"Hey, love birds!" Luke called from the front seat.

"What's up man?" I called back, leaning up from my seat so I could hear him better.

"Weeeee're heeeeere!" He shouted. I pulled back the curtains covering the window beside the table where we sat. The campground was beautiful, each lot big enough for an RV and a couple of tents. A picnic table adorned each lot, along with a charcoal grill. Across the campground, there was a giant pond. It looked like a meteor had struck the ground and caused a massive crater, filled with the deepest blue water I had ever seen. Fish eating the bugs on the surface of the water left tiny ripples filling the otherwise smooth waters. It was going to be a great weekend.

Luke and I scavenged through the campground kitchen, looking for pans and pots to start cooking dinner for everyone. I rummaged through some drawers on the far end of the kitchen, shifting through rusty and dusty pans. A loud clanking sound like an avalanche of metal came from the other side of the kitchen. I looked over my shoulder to see Luke on his back with a pile of pots and pans in his lap.

"I found one," he laughed, clearing the mess off his lap. "Mind giving me a hand getting these things put back up?"

I chuckled, closing the cabinets I had been searching and making my way to Luke. I started picking up the pans and putting them back in the cabinet when he said, "So what kind of jobs are you looking at man?"

Bailey and I had talked so much about my looking for a new job, but I forgot I hadn't told a lot of people about it, and the ones I did I didn't go into great detail. "I really want to go into writing, journalism or communications. You know I've always had a passion for writing. I'm good at crafting words and stories."

"And you're not just good at it man, you're really good. I hope we can work together again one day, that would be badass. I miss you buddy." He lifted himself off the ground and picked up a black cast iron pot and pan. We had stocked up on a lot of beer before we came, five cases to be exact. When Luke started drinking, he tended to get a bit emotional.

"That would be really cool, maybe a job will open at MBEA for something," I said, exploring the possibilities of working with

Luke again in the future. We always had a good time when we worked together. We challenged each other, pushed each other to do better in the workplace.

"Does she know?" He finally asked.

"Not yet." The nerves returned to my stomach. "I... I don't know how to tell her man. What if it scares her off? Makes her afraid of me?"

"I have seen the look in her eyes when she looks at you, the tone of her voice when she's being all lovey dovey with you. I'm telling you man, she's into you. I haven't seen a girl that was this into you, and that's a good thing.

"I see the way you look at her, with this look of hope and love in your eyes, the way your face lights up when you talk about her. You two are as perfect a match as I have ever seen."

"I'm planning on telling her this weekend," I admitted, staring off into space and envisioning the way she looked at me. "Maybe even tonight. I want to tell her, and a part of me feels like she already knows. Dude, the way she looks into my eyes, it feels like she's just reading every little secret I have. Like somehow she can see into my soul, read it, understand it."

B ailey and I had packed a tent to bring with us. We wanted the whole outdoor camping experience, sleeping in a tent under the stars. Having an actual bathroom was a nice commodity though. We finished setting up the tent and crawled inside where we had a double sleeping bag setup.

I slid in first, making sure we had no creatures trying to spend the night with us in the sleeping bag. After I was comfortably in, Bailey slid next to me, rolling over to face me with the pillow under her head. "What's on your mind?" She asked.

This was it, I had to tell her. "Wha- what do you mean?" I stammered.

"You've seemed preoccupied tonight. Not like you're ignoring me or anything, but I can just tell there's something on your mind. You know you can talk to me, right?" She was so astute about the little things like this, she was learning more and more about me and my little quirks. It amazed me how much attention she paid to me, it made me feel like she really cared about me.

"Yeah, I guess there is something," I finally sighed, propping myself up on my elbow and looking down into her eyes. "It's something I've been afraid to tell you, and honestly I'm not quite sure how to tell you. There are... things about me that you don't know yet. I want you to know, it's just..."

She propped herself up on her elbow too, raising her eyes to be even with mine. She gave me that look again, like she was searching for the answers on her own. Her eyes flickered from side to side while looking into mine. "What is it, Clay?"

I took a deep breath and closed my eyes, slowly letting it out. "It isn't something I'm proud of, but it is also something that is out of my control." I opened my eyes again, daring to look into hers, daring to let her in and be vulnerable with her. "I have some... issues. I need to tell you about them before we go any further into this."

"Into what?" She asked, genuinely confused. "You're being so cryptic, Clay, just tell me."

"Into our relationship. I'm bipolar, Bailey, and on top of that I have massive anxiety and depression. I'm on medicine for it now.

I've been trying to find the right combination for a year. I think I finally found one though..."

She leaned in, moving her lips against mine in the middle of my sentence. I cupped the side of her face with my freehand as I felt her lips brushing mine, as my tongue ran across her bottom lip, circling around the top. She pulled back, her eyes closed, and a smile on her face.

"Clay," she said, opening her eyes and fluttering her eyelashes. "Why were you afraid to tell me that?"

"Girls have run from it before. They've been afraid of it, and I get it. Who wouldn't be afraid of it? The constant mood swings, from happy to sad to angry. I'm constantly trying to figure out what's wrong with me. Then there's the stigma behind mental illness and that it means you're crazy or violent. It just isn't easy to open up about something that is viewed in such a negative light."

"And there is a reason I'm lying in this tent with you and not any of those other girls. They weren't right for you. They weren't willing to put in the time to truly get to know you, to learn who you are as a person. They didn't deserve to get to do that, not if they couldn't accept you for you."

"Why are you so perfect, Bailey Childe?"

"I'm far from it, but we're perfect for each other."

I couldn't help but smile as I leaned in, pushing my lips against hers, allowing her lips to fall in between mine. I embraced the touch, heat building in my cheeks as I turned flush. Feeling her lips, working around mine, made everything feel okay again.

The next day, Ally, Bailey, Luke, and I went down to the pond, where we set up on the bank in folding chairs and beach towels spread across the ground. We had a cooler full of beer, a bag full of snacks, fishing poles, and worms. We planned to spend the better part of the day fishing, something Luke and I loved doing together. We always wound up turning it into a competition between us, to see who could catch the biggest fish, or the most fish, or a certain kind of fish, or the first fish. We didn't care, we just liked pushing each other.

"Clay," Bailey called out, her line and hook dangling in front of my face as she turned to face me. "Will you help me put the worms on?"

I smiled at her, leaning away from the dangling hook. I reached into the container full of dirt and pulled out a worm. "Are you afraid of worms?"

"No, I would just rather not have to put them on the hook. That's disgusting," she laughed.

"Do you know how to cast?" I slid the worm on the hook for her.

"How to what?"

"Here, like this," I picked up my rod and reel and turned towards the water. I grabbed the fishing line just before it got to the first hole on the rod, flicking the bail backwards to release the line. In one swoop, I held the rod back and flicked it, letting go of the line as it flew over the water and landed in the water with a simple *bloop.*

"Okay," Bailey said, steadying herself and preparing to cast. She took in a deep breath, grabbing the string and slinging the rod backwards. She thrust the rod forward, sending the rod and reel flying across the pond.

I couldn't help but laugh, she was so adorable. Her face turned red as she looked at me with wide eyes. "I am so sorry," she squeaked.

"Bailey, it's fine. You can help me fish," I smiled at her, extending my rod to her.

"Nope," Luke called, stripping down to his black and blue boxers. "We're all fishing today." He ran to the edge of the pond and dove in, swimming to the middle of the pond where Bailey's rod was still floating.

"Luke!" Ally called out, laughing. "You're nuts! What if there are alligators?"

"I'll just *wrastle* them," he called back in his best Cajun accent. He paddled his way towards the shore. Then he stopped, his head submerged under the water as bubbles floated to the top.

"Shit." I threw my shirt off and ran to the water. I dove into the edge and swam to where the bubbles were steadily forming. Once I got there, I felt something grab my foot and pull me under. I opened my eyes, the water blurring my vision, to see Luke laughing at me under the water.

He propelled himself back up to the top and I followed him. "You asshole," I said, smacking the surface of the water and sending water flying into his face.

"Get in you two!" He shouted to Ally and Bailey.

They looked at one another, unsure of what to do. Finally, Bailey reached down and grabbed the bottom of her white shirt, pulling it over her head. Underneath, she was wearing a black bathing suit top lined with tiny sunflowers. She was stunning, her bare skin exposed to the sunrays and her red hair glimmering in the bright light of the sun.

Ally followed suit, taking her long blonde hair out of a ponytail and letting it fall down her now bare back. She slipped her clothes off, revealing a red and white bathing suit underneath. She was slightly taller than Bailey, around the same size throughout their body, but she was more flat chested.

Bailey took off running and jumped into the pond. Once she was in the warm water, she began swimming out to where I was. She wrapped me in her arms, pulling me closer to her. The water wrapped around our bodies, pushing us closer together, forcing our slick skin to meet. I could feel her bare skin against mine as her stomach rubbed my side, it was cool and soft. She leaned up, planting a kiss on my cheek, and resting her head on my shoulder.

"Thank you, Clay," she said.

"For what?"

"This weekend. It's been so fun. And thank you for telling me last night."

I saw Luke glance at me from the corner of my eye, he was smiling and nodding slightly in approval. He was happy that I was happy, that she embraced me for who I was. How had I gotten so lucky? She was amazing, caring, loving. I just had to make sure I didn't screw it up.

We'll Miss You, Bailey

"Hello?" Josh answered when he finally picked up. It always took him a bit to answer phone calls.

"Hey, Josh, what're you doing?" I asked cheerfully. Josh wasn't just my brother, he was also my longest and most reliable best friend.

Growing up, we had to be. We were each other's support system. Staying at our dad's was tough on both of us. He wasn't the easiest to get along with. He was homeless for a bit, and we would go without eating some days. We got through it, together. If I ever got married, he would for sure be my best man.

"Uh, not much dude, what's up?"

"Let's grab lunch. I want you to get to know Bailey better."

"Yeah man, I'm good with that." I could hear a hint of happiness in his voice. Bailey was the first girl I had introduced him to since my high school ex. My brother's standards for a girl for me was astronomically higher than anyone else's, even my mom's.

"Cool, I'll call Bailey and shoot you the details." We said our goodbyes, and I hung up the phone, immediately dialing Bailey's number.

"Hello?" Her voice sang from the other end of the phone.

"Hey baby," I said, smiling at the sound of her sweet voice. It always seemed to make me smile when I heard her voice, no matter how bad of a day I was having. "Are you doing anything for lunch?"

"Not that I know of, why?" She asked, curiosity in her tone.

"Well, I was going to see if you wanted to get lunch with Josh sometime. I really want you two to get to know each other better. He is my best friend. I know you met at mom's, but I think just the three of us would be better for you two to get to know one another."

"Yay!" She giddied. "I'm so excited to see him." We decided on the when and where and I texted Josh, confirming our lunch.

As I pulled into the parking lot of the sandwich shop, spotting Josh's jet-black Toyota Tacoma sitting on 35 inch tires. I slid in beside him and hopped out the car, standing in the empty space next to my car to try and save it for Bailey.

"Hey man," Josh said, coming out of his truck. Josh was taller than me by a couple of inches, but younger by three years. His brown hair poofed on top of his head and a spotty beard filled in his chiseled face. "Bailey didn't ride with you?"

"Nah, she's got to work after this, so we drove separately," I explained. "She's really excited to see you again."

"I'm excited to see her, too. Mom seemed to really like her. I did too from the little bit we talked. Mom kept talking about her the night she'd met her. Sounds like she is going to be a keeper to me."

I smiled at the thought of Mom liking her that much. Her approval meant the world to me, and I don't think I could be with someone she didn't approve of. The next step was Josh's full approval.

I caught a glance of Bailey's van pulling into the parking lot and heading our direction. I stepped out of the parking space, allowing her room to park. Josh walked over to where I was, eagerly waiting to meet her.

Bailey stepped out of the car. "Hey babe." I wrapped my arms around her, letting them fall over her shoulders and kissed the top of her forehead.

Josh reached out and took Bailey's hand gently, shaking it and smiling at her. "It's good to finally see you again." His eyes glanced towards the van and back at Bailey.

"You too! Clay talks about you all the time. I want to get to know his brother better," Bailey laughed.

Josh had called a couple of times when Bailey and I had been together, and I have a habit of putting my phone on speakerphone. Bailey, being her normal Bailey self, would always talk to him with me.

"Alright you two, I'm hungry," I said, turning and walking towards the sandwich shop.

The two followed behind me, talking like they were old friends. I loved that my family already felt as if she were family. She was truly special.

When we got seated at our table, ordered our drinks and food, Bailey became the first to speak up. "You've got to tell me embarrassing stories of Clay from when you were kids." She playfully looked over at me and nudged my side with her elbow.

Josh laughed, sitting back and stroking his chin while he thought of the most embarrassing thing he could. This was going to be good. "His favorite musician used to be Weird Al, and he thought his theme song was White and Nerdy."

Bailey burst out laughing, leaning over the table. "Seriously, Clay?"

I could feel my cheeks flushing red. "Yes, I was very nerdy back in high school, and I embraced it."

"Oh wait, did he ever show you a picture of him in high school?" Josh asked as he reached in his pocket and pulled out his phone.

"No, I don't think so." She arched her eyebrow in curiosity.

He scrolled through his social media to find a picture of me from high school. He settled on two. First, he showed her a picture of me from switch day, wearing a blonde, curly wig and a blue, green, and red skirt. It was my senior year, I had gone all out.

The second was a picture from my sophomore year, when my hair was down to the small of my back. That one was what got her. She started laughing again and turned to me, "Clay Dabrowski!"

"What?" I laughed, rubbing the back of my neck.

"We never would have talked in high school, you know that right?"

"What do you mean?" I asked, arching an eyebrow.

"I was not into the scene style," she joked.

"On a serious note," Josh spoke up. "He was the best brother I could have asked for. He really was. We didn't always get along, but I always knew he had my back. He may have talked shit to me, but he was the only one who was allowed to. He would protect me from any danger he saw coming my way, even from our abusive dad."

Bailey smiled, looking over at me and taking my hand underneath the table. She worked her fingers into the crevices between mine, gripping my hand in hers. Family was important to both of us, and hearing Josh say that not only made me proud, but I could only imagine it made Bailey happy.

Later that night, my phone rang on my side table. The blaring noise woke me up from much needed deep sleep. I rolled over to see *Kenney Frey* flashing across the screen. What time was it? As I answered the phone, I glanced at the time on the top of the screen, reading 9:45 pm.

"Hello," I said, rubbing my eyes with my free hand.

"Hey. What're you doing?" He asked from the other side of the phone. Kenney and I had gotten pretty close recently, talking more regularly about anything and everything. It was a nice change of pace to be able to befriend Bailey's dad, who she valued so much.

"I *was* sleeping," I said, putting extra emphasis on '*was*'. "I have to open tomorrow."

"Look." He cleared his throat. "We're having a going away party for Bailey next weekend, but it's a surprise. I just wanted to make sure you'd be able to be there."

I felt a smile creep across my face. All I had wanted over the last few weeks was to be accepted by Bailey's parents, to be welcomed into her family. Everything seemed to be falling into place.

"Yeah, of course I'll be there."

"Good, I know Bailey wouldn't want it any other way. And what Bailey wants, Bailey normally gets. Because she's Bailey," he laughed. Bailey told me she was the self-proclaimed favorite child. Her family had a joke that Bailey could and would do anything she wanted to simply because she was Bailey Childe.

She was the youngest of her parents' three kids. She often got what she wanted because she was the baby of the family. Even outside of her family, she had a personality that attracted everyone. It made people love her, respect her, and simply want to help her.

I pulled into the driveway of Bailey's parents' house. There were six cars in the yard that weren't normally there, plus neighbors walking over. I was getting ready to meet *everyone* whether I liked it or not.

Before I could even get out of the car, the heads of every person there turned towards me. It was like they knew who I was, and they were getting ready to pounce. I don't think I had ever met this many people of importance to a girl at once. It was nerve racking.

I took a deep breath, rolling my head side to side to let the pressure crack out of my neck. "Let's do this," I whispered to myself. I got out of the car, greeted with a running hug from Bailey.

"Hey you! I didn't know you were coming!" She said, nearly bouncing on her heels.

"Yeah, your dad wanted me to surprise you." I leaned down and kissed her forehead.

"You made it," I heard Kenney call from across the yard. He made his way over to me, two beers in his hands. He extended his hand, offering me one of the beers.

"No sir, I have to drive home," I said. I wasn't trying to impress him. I just didn't believe in drinking and driving. But then he said something I wasn't expecting.

"Why don't you just stay here tonight so you don't have to drive?" Bailey looked at me, her jaw awry, clearly stunned that Kenney had offered that to me.

"Are you sure? I don't want to impose." I was doing my best to keep my composure.

"Nonsense, you're staying. End of discussion," he said with authority in his voice. "Now take this beer before it gets hot."

I did as he said and grabbed the beer, it wasn't a brand I was a fan of, but I would oblige. I cracked it open, held it up, and clinked the neck of the bottles with Kenney before throwing it back.

He laughed, patting me on the back and walked off leaving Bailey and me to ourselves. I turned to look at her, her lips still curled up into a smile as she bit her bottom lip gently.

"What is it?" I asked with a cheesy grin.

"He likes you, Clay. I told you he would like you," she said, throwing herself into my arms. I draped my arms over her shoulders, resting my hands together in the center of her back.

She looked up at me with her beautiful brown eyes, her eyelashes fluttering with the wind. Her face was one of joy, the corners of her lips running up the side of her face trying to reach the top, her eyes sparkled with happiness. This was what I had always wanted, always needed, and I finally had it. Everything was coming together so perfectly.

"Come on, let's go meet some more of my friends and family." She took me by the hand and led me to the backyard. When we got there, I looked around the yard. It was a fun yard, with trampolines for kids, a tool building, fire pit, and a white Trans Am. I felt an overwhelming feeling wash over me.

There were so many people there, it was intimidating. What if they didn't like me? They could convince Kenney I'm no good for Bailey. What if I made an ass of myself? Maybe I shouldn't be drinking. The thoughts swarmed through my mind like piranhas waiting to strike at any moment and ruin my good mood.

I shook off the negative thoughts, trying to clear my mind and enjoy the night. The first person I met was a bigger man, standing roughly five inches taller than me, his shaggy brown hair fell to his shoulders, and a pair of wire framed glasses circled his green eyes and adorned his face.

"Jack," he said, approaching Bailey and me with his hand extended.

"Clay, nice to meet you, sir," I said, grasping his outstretched hand firmly. He returned the grip like it was a competition.

"Please, call me Jack. I've heard a lot about you Clay. Bailey is like a daughter to me, so you better treat her right." He released my hand and stared me down with eyes full of intent. I could tell he was trying to act intimidating, but he really seemed like a big teddy bear. I would never say that to him though.

"Absolutely, sir. She's everything to me right now and I plan to keep it that way. I want to be a protector and provider, but most importantly I want us to be partners in life."

He stuck his bottom lip out and cocked his head, as his eyebrows perked up. "I think you're going to fit right in, Clay. You seem like you have a good head on your shoulders."

I smiled, nodding in appreciation. So far, so good.

The next person I met was a smaller Hispanic man. He was about my height, but much smaller in size. His salt and pepper mustache matched the mop on his head brushed the sides of his lips, never connecting on the bottom.

"Hey buddy," he said as Bailey and I approached him. "My name's Fernando."

"I'm Clay. Great to meet you, sir," I started.

Kenney came up behind us and laughed. "Enough with the sir stuff. I know you're trying to be respectful, but you're a part of this circle now, no need for formalities."

Fernando chuckled as I turned to face him again. "He's right, Clay, no need for the formalities. If you're part of this group," Fernando waved his hand around the yard above his head. "You're part of this group and we're all family here!"

He held his bottle up in the air, as Kenney and I both raised ours, clanking together the necks of the bottles. As I finished off the last of my beer, a dark-skinned man about my age and height, walked up, handing me another beer.

"Looked like you may need that," he said, reaching out his fist. "Bill. I'm Fernando's son in law."

I reached out, bumping my fist to his. "I appreciate it man." I took the beer from him, popping off the top and taking a swig.

"These old timers have got you cornered, don't they?" he joked, pointing his thumb at Fernando and Kenney. "Come hang out with the cool kids over by the fire. Don't want to end up in a pair of white New Balances and mowing the grass hanging out with these two."

I looked over to Bailey, who nodded her head slightly in agreement. "Yeah, alright." I took Bailey's hand and followed Bill.

We got to a fire pit circled by more people around our age. I recognized Chuck and Anne but wasn't sure about the rest. In addition to the people my age were various small children.

I sat in a foldout chair next to Bill, Bailey taking a seat next to me. The first one to speak up was a guy who looked to be about my age and height, but sported red, curly hair. He must have been Bailey's brother.

"What's up man?" He said. "You must be Clay. I feel bad for you man."

I arched an eyebrow, confused. "For what?"

"For having to deal with Bailey," he said, laughing like a snake's hiss.

"Ignore him, that's my asshole brother Alex. You don't have to deal with him much. He lives in Aynor," Bailey said, rolling her eyes and holding back a slight smile.

"Language, young lady," Alex teased. I couldn't help but laugh, not at Bailey but at Alex. He was going to be an annoyingly funny guy to be around, I could tell. But there would never be a dull moment, I guess.

"How old is your baby," I asked Alex, nodding in the direction of the baby he held cradled in his arms. His complexion was already darker than his dads, a head full of red hair, and the cutest cheeks.

"Just turned one," he picked him up and sat him on his lap, facing the circle of people. Wide-eyed, he looked around at all the people. "His name's Gavin. That one running around with the stick is Laykin, He's three."

"Sounds like you got your hands full," I laughed as Laykin ran up to me.

"Who you?" He said, resting the stick across my lap and pushing his hands into my legs, lifting himself slightly off the ground as he leaned in. His deep brown eyes pierced mine, his gappy smile now turned into a scowl with his eyebrows scrunched up.

"I'm Clay. I'm Bailey's friend," I said, looking down at him with a smile. I loved kids, at one point in high school I had considered becoming a kindergarten teacher. I volunteered at Vacation Bible School for local churches, tutored at the local elementary schools, I just wanted to help kids grow and develop.

"Hers boyfriend?" He scrunched up his nose, almost in disgust. It was cute.

"Yeah buddy, her boyfriend."

He huffed, picking up his stick and jumping in Bailey's lap. "My Bailey," he sternly said, laying his head on her chest and wrapping his arms around her. His glare was almost evil. Bailey reached up, laughing, and ruffled his short brown hair.

"I promise I'm not taking her away from anybody, buddy." I was trying to reassure not only him but everybody around. I didn't want any of her friends or family to feel like I was sneaking my way in to steal her away, because that just wasn't the truth.

Later that night, I curled up beside Bailey on the pull-out bed. It had been a successful night. All of her friends and family seemed to love me. Her brother and I had hit it off, joking around all night and talking about cars. Anne warmed up to me even, as I made her and Chuck laugh throughout the night.

I had something I had to say to Bailey. Something I had been wanting to tell her all night but was never really sure what to say. I may or may not have been a little bit tipsy, but everything that came out of my mouth next was the truth.

"I love you, Bailey Childe," I whispered, her head against my chest as I wrapped my arm around her stomach and pulled her in closer. I kissed the back of her head and continued. "Tonight has made me feel really good. I feel like your family and friends are all accepting of me, like I fit in. That's always been my biggest fear, not fitting in with your family.

"I know how important family is to you, and it is to me too. So being accepted like this, it just reaffirms my love for you and how perfect I feel we are together. It feels so much more real, and tangible. I want to be part of your family one day, not just some guy they used to know and that feels closer and closer all the time. I'm just so lucky to be with you.

"I want you to know Bailey, that I promise to come and visit you at least one weekend every month for the entire time you're away. I'll come more often if I can, but I can promise you that."

Bailey hummed happily, nuzzling her head against my chin. "Clay Dabrowski, you are the sweetest guy I know. And you're not the lucky one, I'm the lucky one."

I smiled, feeling the fluttering butterflies swirling in my stomach. "We're both lucky then." I laid my lips on top of her head and breathed in her sweet scent as I dozed off.

First Day Back

We loaded the last of Bailey's things into her van and my car. I had taken today and tomorrow off to help move Bailey into her college dorm. I wanted to be able to be there for her and help her get settled in, but also, I wanted her to know I was serious about my promise to visit her one weekend a month.

I closed the trunk and turned to Kenney and Maye. "We'll text y'all when we get there, I promise," I said reassuringly.

"We better get a phone call," Maye laughed.

"Of course." I flashed them both a big smile.

Maye came up to me and wrapped her arms around me, and I followed suit. "Thank you," she whispered to me.

I pulled my head back slightly and looked at her, my eyebrows raised in confusion. She chuckled. "Thank you for going with her but also thank you for the way you treat her."

My eyes felt like a dam being pressured with water. That was something I had always wanted to hear, that I was treating someone so well their parents appreciated it. It meant I was doing something right. I smiled at her again. "Of course."

I turned to Kenney, extending my hand to him. He gripped my hand, looking at me sharply.

"Take care of her when you get there tonight. Drive safe," Kenney said, releasing my hand.

"I always will," I promised him.

Bailey said her goodbyes to her parents, long hugs and a few tears shed. We got into our cars and headed off to Spartanburg.

After I set my phone's GPS, I called Bailey.

"Hey stranger," she answered, her voice giddy.

"I missed you already, so I figured talking would make this drive shorter and faster. I'm so happy I'm getting to go with you."

"Me too! Being able to go to sleep with you two nights in a row is going to spoil me," she said, her voice gushing through the phone.

"You're sure it's okay if I stay tonight?" It was an all-girls school, so the dorms weren't coed. I would stick out like a sore thumb if I weren't allowed to be there, being the only male counterpart.

"Yes crazy, it's fine," she laughed through the phone.

W e drove for four hours, on the phone with each other the entire time. It was a chance for us to get to know each other even better, to enjoy each other's presence and soothing voices for as long as possible before I would have to leave her side.

I drove through the town, admiring the beauty. The school grounds were the most beautiful part, a historic college centered in one of the most historic towns in South Carolina. The color in the trees were already shifting from vibrant green leaves to bright yellows and burnt oranges, fluttering from the branches and lining the sidewalks and street curbs, building up in the drains. The older buildings showing their countless memories and stories on the outside with bronze plaques, telling you the countless stories their walls held.

We got out of our cars once we got to the dorms and began unloading them. I looked over to Bailey and asked, "Why here?"

"Converse?" I nodded my head and she continued, "It was the atmosphere. When we came to visit, it was decorated for Christmas, and I loved it. Once I got to the actual tour, it was all so personal. They even sent me handwritten thank you cards when I got home. I knew then that this was the place I wanted to be, a place I wanted to continue my soccer and educational career."

As she finished, Mary came shrieking out of the door of the dorms screaming Bailey's name. Bailey spun around, flinging her arms open as Mary wrapped her in a hug.

Mary stood back, glancing past Bailey and at me. "Oh," she started. "*He's* here."

"Yes, Mary, of course he is. I told you he was coming," Bailey said, almost pleading her not to be mean.

I smiled at Mary. "I'm only here for a day, after tomorrow I'll be gone until next month and she is all yours."

Mary groaned. "Just how often do you plan on being here?"

"At least one weekend a month, maybe more never less." I held my hands up jokingly towards her.

Then her face turned. The furrow of her brows and scrunched up nose disappeared as she started smiling. "He's definitely better than the last one. But we'll see if he can keep his word."

Bailey turned to Mary, looking at her deep in the eyes with reassurance. "He will, I promise."

Mary turned one last time to look at me, and then back at Bailey. "Prove her right, Clay."

"I will," I said with a smile on my face and a look of promise. Then the three of us unloaded the cars and got all of Bailey's stuff into the dorm room.

The room was small, barely big enough for one person much less two. Despite the size, a bed was pushed against each wall with a desk connected to the end. The walls were cinder blocks heavily coated with pale white paint, and the lighting made it even more dull in the place.

"This is home for the next eight months," Bailey groaned, not enthusiastically at all. "In all of its glory."

I wrapped her in my arms, trying to soothe the sadness her voice conveyed. I pulled her into me, our bodies pressed together nearly as one. I laid a kiss firmly on her head, letting my lips linger on the spot.

"I'll make it more interesting for you next time I come up, I have some ideas of how to brighten this place up," I said as I slowly leaned back. I picked her up, playfully throwing her on the bed. I discarded my shirt and followed down after her. I fell on my stomach as she rolled to her side, giggling and looking at me.

"Is that your way of telling me you want to take a nap sir?" She giggled.

I closed my eyes and smiled. "Yes, ma'am, it is." I pulled her into me, resting my chin on her head, and we dozed off.

The sound of the fire alarms shrieking throughout the dorm startled us awake. I rolled off the bed, quickly grabbing my shirt off the ground and throwing it over my head.

"Clay, it's just a test alarm," Bailey groggily said as she rolled out of bed laughing. "They do it every year on the first day."

"Oh," I said, rubbing the back of my neck. "So we don't need to go outside?"

"Oh no," Mary said walking into the room. "You have to go outside, this is a real one. I just came back to get my phone."

"Mary, are the RA's out there?" Bailey asked. Why was she worried about the RA's? It was supposed to be okay for me to be here, wasn't it?

"Yes, they are sweetie, and I don't know how you're going to avoid this one," Mary laughed, almost mockingly.

I looked at Bailey and cocked my head to the side. "Bailey..."

"Okay, so you may *not* be allowed here on the first day," she said, biting her lips nervously. "But you are allowed here during the year! Just... not the first day."

"Bailey," I groaned, following her out the door. "Do I need to leave?"

"Maybe they won't even say anything, sometimes we have RA's who don't give a shit," she said trying to convince herself more than me.

As we got to the exit, I threw my hood over my head and tucked my chin down and pressed my beard to the inside of my hoodie, trying to avoid anybody spotting me. I followed closely behind Bailey, holding onto the tip of her fingers with mine.

We made our way through the crowd of girls forming outside of the building until we got to the other side of the street. Once we got there, I threw the hood off my head and looked at Bailey as she turned to face me. My adrenaline was pumping through my veins as my heart beat against the inside of my chest.

It was an exhilarating feeling, one I hadn't felt in a long time. Bailey was bringing that out of me again, a side of excitement and spontaneity that I had been so badly missing lately.

"Do you think we're in the clear?" Bailey asked Mary as she got to the side with us.

"I don't know, I heard one of the RA's say something about a guy being here. Clay, put your hood back on," Mary said as she slapped my arm, but as the words left her mouth another voice called out from across the road.

"Hey, he can't be here," a tall female said as she walked over to us. She was plumper than the rest of us, her stringy blonde hair flowed down her cheeks, while a pair of thick framed glasses sat on her nose. "No guests on the first night."

"I wasn't staying," I spoke up, trying to formulate an excuse and get out of this predicament. "I've been helping my girlfriend get her stuff put up, we're almost done."

"Doesn't matter, no guests after 8," she said, throwing her wrist in our faces to show us the screen of her smart watch. "You've got to leave, sir."

I wasn't going to push it anymore and risk not ever being able to visit. So I told her I understood and turned to say goodbye to Bailey.

"I'll be back in a month, I promise." I lifted her hands to my lips and kissed each knuckle. When I started towards the parking lot, Bailey chased after me. As I was getting in the car, she was falling into the passenger side.

"You're not going anywhere without me mister," she said, closing the door behind her.

"Bailey, you've got to stay," I pleaded to her.

"Let's just go get something to eat. I have an idea. If you still want to stay." She turned to me. I loved the way she looked with a mischievous smile turned up on her lips.

"Okay, here's the plan," Bailey whispered as she slouched over the restaurant table to get closer to me. "We're going to go in through the back door. The back door leads to the stairwell and there's hardly ever anyone in there. Once we go up to the third floor, my room is only four doors down."

I was impressed at how creative she was getting with this. She really wanted me to stay. "What if we get caught again?" I asked her.

"We'll worry about that if it happens." She looked up into my eyes. I looked into her eyes, trying to read hers like she read mine. All I could see was innocence, pure innocence and I loved it. She would be my anchor, to pull me down from the anxiety highs or up from the depression lows.

"Are you sure you won't get in trouble?"

"I'm not sure, no. I've never done this before, but it'll be fine because I am Bailey Childe." She laughed as she swished her hair with her hand.

I took a deep breath. "Okay, Bailey Childe, let's do it." We finished our food and headed back to the car, heading back to Converse.

While I drove, I took her hand in mine, wrapping my fingers in between hers like vines holding on tightly to a tree. I enjoyed the rush of what we were doing, I could feel the excitement coursing through her veins, so I knew she did too.

"Why are we doing this?" I asked her.

"What do you mean?" She raised an eyebrow, curiosity peeking through in her tone.

"Why're you risking this all for me to stay with you?"

"I'm not letting you drive all the way back home after this long of a day. I'm also not letting you spend money on a hotel. I love you Clay. I'll risk it all for you."

I smiled the biggest I had in a long time. When I pulled into the school grounds, I cut the lights of my car off and coasted down the dark road. We pulled into the parking lot and got out of the car, sneaking through the shadows to the back door.

Bailey went ahead of me, slowly opening the door. As the door opened, the hinges screamed at the top of their lungs. They hadn't been greased all summer, and our ears and plans were paying the price.

Bailey slid in, holding the door in place for me as I made my way in. As the door started to fall shut, the door on the opposite wall started to open. I flung myself out of the door I had just come in through, pressing my back against the brick wall outside.

I stood there silently, waiting for Bailey's signal. My breathing was heavy from the adrenaline, gulping large amounts of air to try and keep calm. The door finally creaked open again and Bailey poked her head out. "Come on," she whispered, waving her hands inside.

I filed in behind her, following her feet bouncing from one step to the next, skipping a few steps here and there with leaps. We reached the second floor and paused, listening to make sure nobody was coming. As soon as we paused, a door from above opened.

I started back down the stairs when Bailey reached out and grabbed my arm, pulling me back to her. "I think that was from the fifth floor, they may not come all the way down."

We hunkered down against the wall, anxiously listening to the echo of one foot on the hard floor, then another, and another. Finally, they stopped, and the sound of a door opening took its place. We stood there for another minute listening for any lingering footsteps.

Hearing none, we took off up the next flight of stairs. This time we picked up the pace and took two steps at once, trying our best to get to the next floor as quick as possible. Once we made it, Bailey headed straight to the door.

She peeked into the hallway, looking around to make sure the path was clear. She turned back to me, a massive grin on her face and said, "Come on, come on!"

I quickly ran to her side, throwing my hood back over my head in case anyone came out. We got to Bailey's door when she realized she didn't have her key. She started knocking rapidly on the door in hopes Mary was in there.

As Mary opened the door, the sound of another door opening started to follow. Bailey grabbed onto my wrist and pulled us through the door, nearly knocking Mary down.

She closed the door back, laughing as she turned to us. "You're learning from me, aren't you Bailey? Back door trick?" Of course it had been Mary who taught her that. Mary seemed to bring out the wild side of the normally calm and cautious Bailey.

Bailey laughed, collapsing on the bed and pulling me down beside her. "Yup, worked like a charm," Bailey smiled as she rolled over to face me.

I reached over and gently stroked the side of her face with the side of my fingers, leaning in to place my nose against hers. "I love you," I whispered.

Bailey fluttered her eyes a few times. "I love you, too."

To New Beginnings

I laid alone on my back in Bailey's twin sized dorm bed. My phone held firmly in my hands as I scrolled through job boards. I quit The Door to find something more in-line with my degree, something I would actually enjoy.

I just couldn't take it anymore. It wore on my body and mind. It was toxic for me, between the constant moving from store to store to their new store two hours away. I would close the new store, drive two hours and sleep for two hours, to wake up and open another store.

They were using me as a district manager, and for less than what the other managers were making, much less, and no benefits like the rest had. They were using me because of my age, and my lack of managerial experience to justify my pay, and I had enough.

Thinking in hindsight, though, I probably should have lined a job up first. But I just couldn't take it anymore. Bailey had finally made me believe I was worth more, made for more.

The door opened and was flooded with Mary and Bailey's laughter. It startled me, almost causing me to drop my phone on my face. I slung my legs off the bed and sat up.

"How was class, girls?" I asked as they entered the room.

"Don't even get me started," Mary said, slinging her backpack on her bed.

"Oh, Mary, stop being dramatic," Bailey laughed, sitting down beside me and wrapping her arm around my waist. I leaned over and kissed the side of her cheek, fluttering my eyelashes against her temples.

"I'm not! That bitch shouldn't have started with me," Mary snapped back, shrugging her shoulders.

"Somebody please tell me what happened," I pleaded in confusion and curiosity.

"Fine," Mary huffed. "We were debating which is more important in helping you lose weight, cardio or strengthening. This BITCH had the audacity to ask me what I knew about exercising. Like I am an athlete at this school. I play soccer for this school. What do you know about exercising, Miss Priss?"

I couldn't help but to laugh, shaking my head. "I think Mary's right on this one Bailey."

"She is?" Bailey asked, whipping her head around.

"I am?" Mary asked, her eyes wide clearly confused that I was agreeing with her. Although, since I had been coming up here so often since I'd left The Door, we had developed a best friend-esque friendship.

"Yes," I laughed. "How dare she ask you what you know about exercising? Sounds to me like she was insinuating something."

"Exactly," Mary said, throwing her hands out towards me and turning to eye Bailey.

"*ANYWAYS*," Bailey exaggerated, rolling her eyes. "How's the job search going, babe?"

"Slow. I've been applying for a lot, but I'm not getting very many call backs," I sighed. "I know I don't have a lot of experience, but I'm a damn hard worker. If I could just get an interview, I could show them who I am and why I'm deserving."

Bailey placed her hands on my face, turning me to face her. "You will find something. You have so much potential and so much heart, that you are going to find something. It may not be right away, and that's okay. Don't give up."

"It just doesn't make sense that entry level positions are asking for three to four years of experience. How am I supposed to get experience if I have to have experience to get experience?"

"Whoa, what did you just say? You lost me at the end," Mary said, laughing at herself.

I smiled a half smile at her, leaning in and pecking Bailey's lips with mine. "I just feel like I shouldn't have left without a job lined up."

"Baby," she started. "We've talked about this. You were comfortable leaving because you had enough saved up to last you the rest of your lease. You have five months, you're going to find something by then."

"Clay, she's right," Mary chimed in. "Everything I've seen you do, everything you've put your mind towards, you give it 110%. Some lucky employer is going to find you."

I looked over at my phone as it started ringing. A number with my area code was calling, but it wasn't one I was familiar with. Probably a spam call.

"Hello?" I said.

"Is this, Clay Dabrowski?" A lady's voice came from the other end.

"It is."

"Hi Clay, this is Lori with Carolina Hospice Care. You applied for our part time communications coordinator position?"

"Yes ma'am, I did," I said, smiling and looking over at Bailey. She looked back at me and cocked her head to the side, confused.

"Well, we wanted to see if you could come in for an interview this Thursday," Lori said as she typed in the background.

"Yeah, of course. What time?" My smile widened as the excitement built.

"Let's say 10:30 in the morning."

"I'll see you then, thank you so much!" I said as we hung up the phones. "I've got a job interview!"

"Yay!" Bailey cheered, wrapping her arms around my neck. She placed little kisses up and down my neck. "I told you something would come."

I was up early the day of the interview. I had a list of questions prepared, and I wanted to read over all my notes on the company. I wanted to be prepared to impress the interviewers. I also wanted to look professional, so I used the extra time to freshen up.

I took the longest shower of my life, enjoying the streams of scorching water flowing over my head. I closed my eyes, reflecting on my experience and the information I had ready for the interviewers. I just wanted to relax before the interview.

When I finished, I picked out my finest navy suit. It wasn't much, but it fit me well. I wrapped myself in my white button up shirt. I had a navy bow tie to match the suit. I even pulled out my Masonic cufflinks. I looked at myself up and down in the mirror. I was kind of impressed with myself.

I pulled out my phone and snapped a mirror picture, sending it to Bailey for her approval. Almost as soon as the swoosh of a successfully sent message left my phone, it dinged with a message from Bailey.

"You look so good baby!" The message said.

"So I have your approval then?"

"You always have my approval hot stuff."

I walked out of the interview, a smile spread from cheek to cheek. I loosened my bow tie with one hand as I got in the car, bringing the engine to a roar with my other. The interview had gone so well. They were impressed with how much I knew about the company and with my eagerness to display my skills.

I called Bailey as I took off down the road. "Hey babe!" She answered cheerfully. "How did it go? Tell me all about it."

"It went so good! They loved me, I blew them away with the research I did. They said I am ahead of the other candidates right now, and I'm definitely coming in for a second interview next week!"

"That's awesome! I'm so happy for you baby. I knew you could do it," she said. "You worked so hard to make sure you knew all about the place. I'm going to need your help when I start preparing for interviews. What day is your interview next week?"

I paused for a minute. I was supposed to stay with her next Wednesday, but the only day they had open was Thursday at eight in the morning. That would mean a four in the morning departure time at the latest.

"Thursday at eight in the morning," I finally said.

"Do not worry about coming up here Wednesday! Your interview is far more important. We can see each other another day."

"Bailey, we already bought tickets to the fair for that night, and we can't get a refund. Plus, I promised you I would, and I intend to keep that promise."

"Then how are you going to make it back in time?" She paused. "You are not leaving at five in the morning, Clay Dabrowski."

"You're right, that's not the plan." I smirked and half chuckled into the phone, imagining her face.

"Okay, then I'm listening."

"I'll leave at four, so I have a few extra minutes for traffic."

"Fine," she huffed. "You're good at that."

"Good at what?"

"Being very careful with your choice of words. I love it. It keeps me on my toes, you always get so technical. I don't know, one of your little quirks that I love I guess."

The following Wednesday, Bailey and I sat in the little compartment of the ferris wheel. I looked over at her, her beautiful eyes scanning the horizon of the fairgrounds. People screaming on the rides and people laughing and talking filled the air. The brightly colored lights throughout the fairgrounds lit up the night sky. The smell of popcorn, funnel cakes, and sausage dogs filled our senses.

I wrapped my arm around Bailey's shoulders and pulled her in closely. She rested her head on my shoulder as she scooted over to me. I took her hand in mine, intertwining our fingers.

She nuzzled my shoulder and said, "Thank you, Clay."

I rested my head on hers, wanting to be connected to her in every way I could. To be closer to her. "For what, my love?"

"For coming up here today." She lifted her head up slowly and looked at me. "Tomorrow is such an important day for you, yet you're here. You're with me."

"Of course I'm with you, Bailey." I took her other hand in my now free arm. "I will always keep the promises I make to you. I've been studying more, doing some writing exercises to keep me on my toes. I'm ready for this, and I'm ready for you."

The ferris wheel came to a halt as we got to the top. I looked into her eyes, as she stared back into mine. She was reading me again, I could tell by the way she looked at me. I slowly closed my eyes, turning my head to the side, and leaned in.

Our lips met and I moved my hand to her waist and side. She brought her hands up and locked them behind my head, pulling me further into her kiss. Our lips locked, her bottom falling in between mine. My tongue met hers.

I pulled back, still biting my lip and opened my eyes. "Always," I said to her.

"Forever."

Around seven thirty the next morning, I pulled into the parking lot of Carolina Hospice Care. I made pretty good time, even stopping for a couple of energy drinks and cups of coffee along the way. I was tired to say the least, but last night had been worth it. Bailey was worth it.

Spending all that time with her at the fair, just enjoying being with one another, was so nice. I loved our dates because we always seemed to fall more and more in love during every single one. Our connections grew stronger.

I finally got out of the car and headed into the building, where I greeted the receptionist. "Good morning, Ms. Rita, it's good to see you again."

"Hello, Clay," she said stunned. I had been taught to treat everyone with the same respect, so I always would give it to the receptionist as well. Not many people do that on job interviews, it's a rarity. They're the gatekeepers to the business, the first impression. Make your first impression on them and they can very well influence the decision. "I'm so glad to see you again. I told them I liked you a lot after the first time."

"Thank you, Ms. Rita. That means a lot." I smiled my kindest smile at her.

"They're waiting for you in the conference room, whenever you're ready, dear."

I took a deep breath, with my briefcase in hand I started off to the conference room. I got to the large wooden double doors, a square of metal with a handle sprouting from it placed on the insides of the doors. I pulled them open, walking in expecting to see the same four people as last time.

The only person in there was the VP of Marketing and Communications. The big boss. I felt my chest start to thunder, and my nerves kicked up. I was better in crowds than one on ones.

"It is a pleasure to see you again, Mr. Teal," I said, extending my hand to him before sitting down.

He stood, gripping my hand and smiling. He was former military, so he had near perfect posture and his grip was firm. He had broad shoulders and a bald head. He was intimidating.

"Please, the pleasure is all mine," he said, sitting back in his seat and motioning for me to sit down. "So today's interview is just going to be an assignment. I'm going to give you a couple of scenarios, and you're going to draft a press release for each one."

"Yes, sir, sounds good." I was almost overly eager. I had been practicing my writing skills for this very reason. I loved writing. It had been a passion of mine since I had been a little boy. I was excited that I'd finally get a chance to show off my skills, to show them what I could bring to the table.

He stood up and walked over to a computer on a desk in the corner of the room. He pulled the chair out. "You'll work here. Everything is pulled up already. All you have to do is read the scenarios and write the release in the box below. When you're done, you can hit submit and leave, no need to wait for us to come back."

I got to the computer and sat down. I focused intently on the screen. As I stared at the screen, the words started to blur together, and my eyes got heavy. The lack of sleep was starting to catch up to me. My head felt like it was full of lead as I started to fall forward in my seat.

I caught myself and blinked my eyes a couple of times, my vision becoming a little clearer. I read the first scenario three times, struggling to put together a coherent sentence. The lack of sleep was really weighing on me. I struggled.

Then my anxiety struck like a viper. *You're not good enough for this place. You can't even do this simple thing. Whatever you write will be shit. They're going to laugh at your stuff. You're a failure.* The thoughts swarmed my mind, consuming me.

"No you're not," Bailey's voice rang in my head as a vision of her beautifully rounded, pale, and freckled face appeared in my thoughts. *"You've got this, baby. I know you do. I'm so confident in you. You've got to be confident in yourself."*

Yeah, I did. I pushed away the negative thoughts, focusing on the scenarios again. The juices flowed as my fingers worked across the keyboard like a pianist. Hearing and seeing Bailey had been my way of coping with anxiety lately. When I was having a panic attack or near breakdown, her voice and face would appear in my head. She would reassure me like she always does. She soothed the restless beast within.

The next week I sat in the mall food court with Bailey and Mary when my phone rang. It was from Carolina Hospice Care. Bailey looked down and back up at me wide eyed, and she smiled at me.

"What're you waiting for, Clay? Answer it," she said, playfully slapping my arm.

"What if they're calling to tell me I didn't get the job?" I fidgeted in my seat as my nerves grew and my muscles tensed.

"Then on to the next one, Clay," Mary said, grabbing the phone. "Now you talk, or I do."

She pressed the answer button and held it in front of my face. I swiped it out of the air and put it to my ear. "Hello?"

"Clay, this is Lori from Carolina Hospice Care. Is now a good time?"

"Yes, ma'am," I said, gulping down the giant lump that had taken residence in my throat.

"So we want to offer you the position of our part time communications coordinator," Lori said as she went into the specifics of the position. She explained the pay, the benefits, my primary duties, and when I could start.

"Yes, I accept," I was finally able to say. I smiled and looked at Bailey. The happiness in her eyes wasn't what caught me. It was the pride I saw. I was making her proud.

We hung up the phone, and I turned to look at Bailey and Mary. "I got the job!" Bailey screamed in excitement, jumping out of her seat and running to me. She wrapped her arms around me, nearly tipping us backwards in the chair.

"I'm so happy for you, Clay. I knew you would find something. Let's go somewhere for dinner tonight, my treat." She whispered into my ear as she held tightly onto me.

"I'm coming too, and I'm paying for both of you," Mary interjected. Bailey and I laughed together as she let go of me and turned around.

"Of course, Mary," I said, my smile still spread across my face. "I want to celebrate with two of my favorite people."

In all the romcoms the guy always does the extravagant surprises for the girl. Yeah, I always thought that was the coolest. It felt like a beautiful display of affection. I wanted to give that to Bailey as much as I could while she was away.

"Hey, Mary," I said when she answered the phone. "I need a favor."

"Mmmk?" The skepticism in her voice made it even more difficult for me to muster the courage to ask. I hardly ever asked anyone for a favor, and I don't think I'd ever asked Mary for one.

"I want to surprise Bailey this weekend. I'm headed there now."

"Okay, I won't say anything." She assured me, sincerity in her tone.

I hesitated into the phone. "No, I need you to do something for me."

"Oh great, what is it, Clay? What cheesy thing are you getting ready to do?" She knew me so well.

"Can you take her out when I'm about thirty minutes away, go to the mall or something. Take your car."

"Why my car?" The skepticism returned to her voice.

"Because I want to be waiting at her van with balloons and Oreos when y'all get there. I'll even bring some for you, Mary," I laughed.

"Fine, I'll help you. But you better bring me a whole box of Oreos."

"Deal."

Once I was about thirty minutes away—and after stopping to buy another box of Oreos—I called Mary again.

"What, Clay?" She said.

"I'm thirty minutes out. I'll text you when I get everything to-gether."

"I'm taking her to get her nails done, so you've got some time."

"How long does it take you to get your nails done?"

"Well first we have to stop and get coffee, then we have to go to the mall, then we stop at some of the stores on our way to the nail salon..." Mary began rambling.

"Okay, I get it," I interjected. "I'll have about thirty minutes."

"Make it an hour." What was I supposed to do for an hour? Flowers. I would get her flowers.

I pulled into the parking lot, lucking out with an empty parking spot beside Bailey's van. I hoped it wasn't Mary's. I shuffled out the car, reaching into my back seat and pulling out the stuff I'd bought. I threw the two boxes of Oreos on the hood of my car.

I blew the balloons up by mouth, two yellow and one blue. I tied them off with the string, attaching each yellow one on the side mirrors and the blue one on the antenna.

I had a bouquet of sunflowers tied together with burlap laid across her windshield. I placed the cookies underneath the flowers, presented nicely for her. I pulled out my phone and texted Mary.

"On the way," she said.

I stood there anxiously, swaying from foot to foot. I felt the butterflies in my stomach. Was it too much? Not enough? What if she hates sunflowers? Or is she allergic to them? Shit, maybe I should take those away.

Too late for changes now. Mary's car pulled into the parking lot and I looked up. I clearly saw Bailey's confused, yet happy face. Her wide smile grew as she cocked her head, her eyebrows creeping up. Then the sparkle in her eye sealed the deal.

Mary parked her car, and Bailey jumped out, running across the parking lot and jumping into my arms. I reached down and rested my hand on the small of her back as I pulled her in for a kiss.

"That's my parking spot!" Mary yelled.

I sat on the couch at Kenney and Maye's house, smoking a cigarette with Kenney. We had started hanging out after Bailey had left. It was fun hanging out with him, just sitting around talking about life.

Turned out Kenney and I shared some of the same struggles with our mental health, so he understood where I was coming from. We shared an interest in working on cars, too. He would help me with the Challenger when I gave it upgrades. We were getting along really well, and I loved it.

"So how about the white Trans Am in the backyard?" I asked, taking a long drag off the cigarette.

"What about it?" Kenney looked over at me with curiosity sprawled across his face.

"What's wrong with it? I'll help you get it running again."

"Well, to start with it needs a new engine," Kenney laughed.

"What if," I said, leaning up in my chair. "We get it fixed up and give it to Bailey for Christmas. The van is on its last leg. There were so many lights lit up on the dash when I went up there that it looked like a plane's cockpit."

Kenney stroked his chin, biting the corner of his lip. He finally looked back over at me. "How about you fix it up for her and give it to her for Christmas? I'll help you work on it where I can, but you decide on everything else."

"You want me to give it to her?"

"Yeah. You take care of all the costs. It's yours to give."

"Fair enough," I said, leaning back in my seat and taking another drag off the cigarette, the ember at the end growing and glowing.

"I have a request." Kenney turned his head slowly and faced me with a stone-cold look.

"I'm listening?"

"I don't want Bailey slacking off on her exercises with you being up there so much," he said, taking a hit of his cigarette. "I need you to promise me you won't let her get behind, make sure she's following her workouts her coach gave her."

"Absolutely, I promise."

"And look, Bailey's having a hard time," Kenney said, turning back to the tv. I nodded slowly, knowing that Bailey had been struggling in her classes. "We're going to see her this weekend to watch her scrimmage game. Why don't you come along and surprise her?"

"Yeah," I smiled. "That sounds good. I've been missing her anyways."

We pulled into the parking lot of Bailey's dorm, where I hopped out and walked down the road. I threw my hoodie over my head. It was getting cold outside back home and even colder here.

We had two surprises for Bailey. Not only did I come, but so did her nephew Laykin. We wanted to surprise her with him, and then I would come up behind her and be there to surprise her again. It was Kenney's idea.

Bailey was extremely close to her nephews. She loved them like they were her own kids, helping to take care of them after their mom left. When she was around them, she was always laughing and playing. She prided herself in being the cool aunt.

I stood back a bit, hiding behind a bush as I watched Bailey walk out of the door. When she spotted Laykin, she took off running towards him, scooping him up in her arms. She turned back to face her parents, and I took the opportunity to sneak from the bush.

The closer I got to her, the more I just wanted to run and grab her. Things had been rough mentally for me lately. I was shouldering a lot of stress from my new job and depression phases were taking their toll.

I finally got behind her as she got ready to turn around. When she turned around, I stood out in front of the building. Her eyes grew wide, as the edges of her lips turned up. She took off running, almost tackling me. She wrapped her arms around my waist.

"You didn't tell me," Bailey said looking up at me, her arms still wrapped around my waist.

"You don't tell people when you're going to surprise them silly, then it isn't a surprise." I leaned in and kissed her lips. I brushed my lips against hers, pulling on her bottom lip and letting go quickly.

I pulled my head back, biting my lip and smiling at her.

"I love you," she sighed, leaning into me again.

The next day we left the hotel room we'd all stayed in the night before. When we got there, Kenney, Maye, Laykin, and

I walked down to the soccer field to watch Bailey play. Maye had Laykin in her arms and Kenney carried the diaper bag. I had my aviators over my eyes, staring across the field. I hadn't been to a soccer match since I was five.

"So can you two help me understand what's going on during the match?" I asked hopefully.

Laykin whipped around in Maye's arms, looking at me. "I help." He smiled, his two front teeth missing making the smile even more loving.

"Sounds good, buddy," I laughed.

He started kicking his legs to get Maye to put him down. When she did, he took off running and jumped into me. I caught him by his sides, picking him up and turning him around to put him on my shoulders.

He started laughing and clapping when he landed safely on my shoulders. "Do again, do again!"

I laughed again. "No, buddy," I said. "Not right now. Later, I promise."

He crossed his arms placing them on top of my head and putting his chin in the middle. "Fine."

We got to the soccer field and Maye pulled out a blanket. She laid it across the bleachers before sitting down. Kenney went to the edge of the field to stand, so I followed after him with Laykin still on my shoulders.

"What is a forward?" I asked Kenney as I walked up beside him.

"Bailey! Bailey play forward," Laykin said from above my head.

"That's right, buddy," Kenney said. "Their main objective is to score goals Clay. They're the offense essentially."

The girls ran out onto the field, Bailey in front of us. She looked over at us and smiled. Laykin shouted from my shoulders, "Love you, Bailey!"

The official blew the whistle, and the ball went into play. It went from girl to girl as Converse moved the ball down the field. It landed at Bailey's feet on the right side of the field, and she took a shot, kicking the ball in a line drive through a hole between two defenders and just out of the goalies reach to the left.

"Gooooooooooal!!!!!" Laykin yelled. Bailey looked over at us and smiled, running to the sideline in celebration.

"I love you, guys," she said when she got there.

"We love you too, now get back out there," Kenney said, shooing her with his hand.

She looked at me and I mouthed "I love you." She peddled backwards waving at us as she got back into position and ready to play again.

I had been looking for engines for the Trans Am. It was the first step in getting the car running, but also the most expensive. I didn't have the money to get a new engine; I was looking for a used one.

Scrolling through my phone, I finally came across one in my price range. I immediately placed a bid of three hundred dollars on the online auction site. After the green check mark appeared on the screen confirming the bid, I switched over and called Kenney.

"Hello?"

"Hey, I just placed a bid on a motor. It came out of a newer year model, but it's compatible," I said, diving right into it.

"When will it be here?"

"The bidding ends tonight, so assuming I win it says estimated delivery is next week. I was hoping I could have it delivered to your house."

"Yeah, of course. We've got an engine hoist we can use. We'll keep the car and engine in the garage, Bailey never goes in there."

"Perfect." I smiled. Everything was falling in place. I was going to give Bailey the best Christmas ever.

Kenney and I sat in the garage, taking a cigarette break from working on the Trans Am when my phone rang. Bailey's name flashed across the screen, and I answered the phone.

"Hello?"

"Hey, baby, what're you doing?" Bailey asked.

"Sitting here with your dad."

"*My* dad? Why're you with my dad?" She asked, a tone of curiosity creeping up in her voice.

I chuckled a little before continuing. "Your dad and I have been hanging out a lot since you left."

"Oh really?" There was a hint of happiness replacing the curiosity in her tone.

"Yes, ma'am," I said. "We just sit around talking, watching tv, working on my car, whatever."

"That's so good to hear, baby." I could practically see the smile on her face shining through in her tone through the phone. "I wanted to see if you wanted to go to a wedding with me this weekend. My boss for my internship at Spartanburg Health and Fitness is getting married."

"Bailey, I would love to be your date." I smiled to myself. "I also need a date to a former coworker's wedding next weekend, would you come with me?"

"I think I can make that work for you, handsome."

After we said our goodbyes, I turned to Kenney who raised his eyebrow. "What was that about?" He asked.

"We've got two weddings to go two, so the next two weekends I'm going to have to take time off working on the car," I said, sitting back down.

He turned to look at me, one eyebrow raised above the other. "Don't get any ideas yet champ."

"Nope, that isn't even on the radar yet."

"**H**ow do I look?" I asked, turning from my reflection in the mirror to Bailey coming out of the dorm's bathroom. I wore my finest black suit, a white shirt, and a red bowtie accenting the suit. "This bowtie feels tight."

"Oh, look at you, hot stuff," she whistled, walking towards me. She wore a blue dress that fit her form perfectly, rolling over her chest and hips like beautiful ocean waves. Her hair was curly, a single curly tendril sneaking down each side of her face and down to her chin like little flirty strands. She was so beautiful.

"Yeah?" I asked, still tugging at my overly tight bowtie.

"Come here," she laughed. I obliged and walked to her, my fingers stuffed between my neck and the shirt collar. When I got to her, she turned me around and flipped my collar up, tugging at the edges of the bowtie, trying to loosen it for me.

I gagged as she pulled, nearly choking me. "Whoops, sorry," she teased. I could tell in her voice she definitely meant to do that. She continued playing with the sides of the bowtie, pulling one side, and then the other to even them out. Tightening, then loosening. Until finally, it was perfect.

"I can breathe!" I said, throwing my hands in the air dramatically.

"Oh, stop being dramatic." She playfully slapped my arm, laughing.

"You know you love it." I turned towards her and cupped her face in my hands. "I'm so excited to get to meet more of your friends."

She closed her eyes, resting her face in my hands. "They'll love you. I'm sure of it." She opened her eyes and looked into mine.

Mary burst into the room, throwing a bag on the floor and falling onto her bed with a belly flop moaning.

"Everything okay?" I asked her.

"No," Mary bluntly stated. "I can't find anything I like for Denise's wedding. I look fat in everything."

"Shut up," Bailey laughed, throwing a pillow at her.

"I'm serious! Look at all these dresses, none of them fit right," Mary snapped back, pouring the contents of her bag across the bed.

"There's five dresses there, Mary. You have at least fifty in your closet," I said, nodding my head towards her overflowing closet. "Just choose another one."

"You don't get it, Clay. You aren't a girl," Mary huffed back.

"I'm a guy, I know what looks good in a guy's eyes. And that *is* your goal, isn't it? To meet a cute guy at the wedding? Maybe one of the groomsmen if you're lucky."

She glared across the room at me as her cheeks flushed a vibrant red, nearly the color of Bailey's hair. "Yes." She crossed her arms and pouted her lips.

"Suck it up, buttercup. Go pick out another couple of dresses and let us see them."

She stood, sulking, and made her way to her closet. She shut the door behind her to change her clothes. When she finally came out—a good fifteen minutes later—she was adorned in a sparkly red strapless dress. The dress ran down past her feet, trailing behind her. It showed off just enough cleavage without being too revealing. "Well?" She asked, tapping her foot.

"I love it!" Bailey said, clapping her hands together.

I pushed out my bottom lip, the look of impress imprinted on my face. "If there are any single guys there tonight, you'll be the first one they notice."

"Really?" Mary asked, the corners of her lips slowly inching higher. "It isn't too much? Too tight?"

"It's perfect, Mary," Bailey said, leaning her head against me.

We arrived at the wedding venue, a quaint venue tucked away in the historical district of Spartanburg. The outside looked like nothing more than a brick storefront. The windows were wide with reflective tint to keep from seeing inside. When we pushed open the black door, we were transported into a beautiful, magical ballroom.

The bright lights shimmered on golden paint adorning the walls, reflecting in the cedar-colored hardwood floors. Tables lined each side of the room, draped in deep red tablecloths and fine china. There were a few people walking around, picking at hors d'oeuvres and drinks.

I linked arms with Bailey and walked over the threshold, Mary close behind. I leaned over to Bailey and whispered, "Do you know anybody here?"

She quickly scanned the room, searching for anybody she may have known. "Not yet, but I know of at least two other soccer girls who intern there that are coming."

We made our way to a table, claiming our seats with Mary and Bailey's purses on the table and my jacket draped around the back of a chair. Bailey slid her coat off, revealing her blue dress and her figure. She was stunning. It made me wonder what she would look like in a wedding dress.

"Mmmm," I purred as the jacket left her body. I bit the bottom of my lip, looking her up and down, from her black shoes to the top of her radiant red hair. "You look so good."

Bailey threw me an awkward wink, and tried another one, and another, and another. "Confession time," she said, leaning into me. "I don't know how to wink."

I leaned back, looking at her. "Seriously?"

"Nope, watch." She followed with several more very bad attempts at winking. "Nothing."

"I'll teach you." I playfully winked one eye, immediately followed by a wink with the other, and then back to the other. "I don't know how to whistle, if that makes you feel better."

"Yes you do." She stared back at me with disbelief sprawled across her face.

"Nope, watch." I pursed my lips together and tried to whistle. All that came out sounded like air being let out of a tire. I inhaled and tried again. "See, nothing."

"Oh my, Clay, oh my. I'll have to teach you how to whistle."

"What're we whistling?" A voice came from behind us. I turned around to see a Hispanic girl about Bailey's size. Her black hair was curled up on the ends, reaching past her shoulders and resting on her chest. She had the brightest and whitest smile I had ever seen.

"Rosa!" Bailey screamed, throwing her arms around the girl. Rosa was her big sorority sister. She had been Bailey's mentor since she'd been a freshman and Rosa a junior. "Clay, this is Rosa!"

I put on my biggest smile as I reached out my hand. "Hi Rosa, it's so good to meet you. Bailey has told me so much about y'all's adventures."

She turned to look at me, giving me a death stare. Another friend who was going to stare me down. Bailey's friends had a running theme so far.

Then her face switched, and her smile formed as she threw her arms around me. Startled, I almost fell off balance when she brought me in for a hug. I awkwardly reached around and tapped her back, unsure of what was happening.

"I'm a hugger, get used to it," she said, releasing me from her bear hug and looking back at Bailey. "I can't believe this is the first time I've met him, Bailey."

"I know! You're always so busy or out of town when he's here," Bailey laughed. "Why don't you sit with us tonight? You can really get to know him."

"For sure!" Rosa said, throwing her purse onto the table beside my chair. Oh boy.

"So," I said, changing the subject. "Why don't we go get some food. I saw finger sandwiches somewhere."

The ceremony was beautiful, but the after party was the best part. I grabbed a beer from the open bar, walking back to my seat. I sat down beside Bailey, leaning over and planting a kiss on her cheek.

"Hey handsome," she said.

"Hey you." I smiled at her.

The song in the background switched from an upbeat dance song to a slow dance song. Bailey hopped out of her seat, reaching her hand out to me. "Dance with me."

"But," I started, trying to come up with an excuse to get out of dancing. I had nothing. "I just got this beer."

"Clay, come on! It'll be cold when we get back."

"Fine," I huffed as I took her hand and walked with her. I hadn't slow danced with a girl since my high school sweetheart, but I hated it.

I put my hands on the side of her waist and she draped her arms around my shoulders. We swayed back and forth together, moving with the rhythm of the music.

"I love you, Bailey Childe. Always."

She looked at me with this relaxed look, one of pure amazement. Her wide eyes sparkled underneath the lights. "Forever." She relaxed her form, leaning into me with her head pressed on my chest. She wrapped her arms around me as we swayed. "Clay Dabrowski, you are something else."

I walked out of the bathroom of my apartment headed back to my room. I was dressed in a black suit, a blazing red shirt underneath, and a black bow tie wrapped around my neck.

Brian walked out of his room, dressed in a similar suit, but a white shirt and black long tie. "Looking dapper," he said to me.

"You're not too shabby yourself, bud," I chuckled. Brian, Janet, Bailey, and I were all riding together to our old coworker Andrew's wedding. Both Brian and Janet had worked with him longer than me.

Bailey came out of my room, wearing a forest green dress that flowed down her body. Her hair tied up in a bun with a tightly wound braid wrapped around it. She was so damn beautiful. She always was.

"You two are looking sharp," Bailey said, letting out a whistle, then trying to wink at me.

Janet shuffled out behind Brian wearing a bright blue dress that fit well around her slim body. Her stringy brown hair straight down her back. "We're a good looking crew."

Bailey and I sat around the fire in the vacant lot across from the church where the wedding ceremony had taken place. It was your typical southern Baptist church, a white steeple and bell tower sprouting from the pointed roof. The after party was more of a bonfire. We all sat around the fire, drinking and having a good time.

Janet ran over to us, already drunk, tugging on Bailey's dress. "It's time for the bouquet toss Bailey, you've got to come! Clay you've got to be there for the garter toss."

"Yeah man, if I'm doing it you're doing it," Brian said coming in behind Janet and resting his hand on the small of her back. I rolled my eyes, standing up and extending my hand to Bailey. She took my hand in hers and followed behind me to the bouquet toss.

"Come on, Bailey," Janet said, taking Bailey's hand from mine and leading her out to the crowd of girls. "If you catch it, give it to me. I've been trying to get Brian to propose for the longest time."

"I can still hear you," Brian said, his hand cupped to his mouth.

"Good!" Janet yelled back.

The stunning blonde bride in her flowing white wedding dress made her way to the front of the crowd of girls, a bouquet filled with roses and lilies in her hand. I glanced out at Bailey, a wide smile spread across her face as her and Janet joked. The bride turned around and the music played. She threw her body forwards, jerking herself back upright and sending the flowers soaring through the air.

Girls reached up in hopes of grabbing it, but it was just out of reach of their fingertips. The bouquet was headed right to Bailey's chest. She threw her arms up, wrapping them around the bouquet like she had just caught a football. Groans emitted from the other girls as Bailey looked at the flowers in her hands, shoving them to Janet who happily took them.

"Ha!" Janet yelled out as she walked back to Brian and me. "I got it, you have to propose now."

"Bailey caught it. She's the one who gets the proposal. You were given it, that doesn't count," Brian jested.

"Whoa, whoa, whoa," I interjected. "Ain't no proposal coming anytime soon."

"If you catch the garter, you're obligated to marry her. You know that, right?" Brian elbowed my side.

I elbowed him back, a little harder than he did me. The groom made his way out to where the bride had been moments ago, so Brian and I walked out to the much smaller group of guys. "You love her, don't you?" Brian asked once we got to the back of the crowd.

"I do man, she's everything I've ever needed. Not just wanted but needed. She makes me happy. She helps me during my dark times. She's helped me to become a better person."

"I can tell. I'm happy for you man," Brian said, patting me on the back.

The music for the garter toss ramped up, the speakers around the group of guys filling our ears with the upbeat music. The groom took the garter and wrapped it around a football. He ran further out, turning around and focusing on the crowd. He reared his arm back, propelling it forward and letting go of the football. It soared through the air, but none of the guys were reaching for it.

It was coming straight at me. Of course it would, why wouldn't it? I shrugged my shoulders and took a couple of steps back, catching the football right in front of my chest. Brian started laughing, his hand holding his side and buckling over in laughter. "Looks like you've got to marry her now," he said in between laughs.

Marriage was the furthest thing from my mind, but the idea of marrying her crept into my mind. I could see her in a flowing ivory dress, her hair pinned up and wrapped around her head, a bouquet of flowers in her hand as she walked down the aisle. I couldn't help but to smile. I knew it was in the future, but I could see it and it made me happy.

Going, Going, Gone!

A few weeks later, Josh and I sat in a local wing place waiting to order food. It was becoming a regular thing for us to come here two or three times a week and just talk as our way of brotherly bonding. Ever since I'd came clean to Josh about my mental illnesses, he had been a lot more understanding and wanted to spend more time with me. Turned out, he had some problems of his own. We'd gone years without telling each other, afraid of what the other may think.

"So," Josh said after the waitress took our orders and menus, leaving the table. "Your senior year was fun when we got to play together on varsity."

"Yeah, it was," I said, smiling and reminiscing on my high school days.

I tried out for the baseball team from my freshman year all the way to my senior year. I'd finally made it my senior year, probably more so out of pity than actual skill. I had never played organized baseball, but Josh was one of the best players our town had ever seen. Practicing with him, helping him, had made me a better player. For someone who'd never played before, I had done relatively well with my limited opportunities.

"What do you think about joining a rec league for slow pitch softball?" He leaned forward with anticipation.

I paused a minute, mulling over what he just said. It would do me good to get back out on the field, to be out and active more. Bailey had been encouraging me to get out more and be more active. She challenged me, pushed me to do and be better. I had to keep up with her when we played for fun anyways. "Yeah, that would be fun. Like the good ol' days."

"Exactly!" Josh slapped the table and threw his hands out in excitement. "A couple of guys at work are forming a team and asked me if I wanted to play. I told them the only way I would play is if you played, too."

"Let's do it, man," I said, excitement creeping into my tone. I reached my hand across the table and Josh clasped my hand. We shook in agreement. I was getting back on the diamond.

L ater that night, my head was deep in the engine well of the Trans Am when Kenney spoke. "So what else do you have planned for this thing?"

I popped my head up, banging it against the hood of the car. "Shit," I whispered to myself, rubbing the top of my head. "Well, I was thinking of putting new headlights and taillights to give it a blacked out look. Maybe run a couple of racing stripes from the front to the back. Probably throw on some little exterior parts here and there to make it look good."

"What about speakers?" he asked.

"Yeah, I'm going to change the door speakers and upgrade them with better speakers with more bass."

"Why don't you just remove the back seats and replace it with subwoofers?"

I walked to the driver's side door and opened it, peeking inside of the car and peering into the back. We could take out the back seats and build a custom box. "You think she'll like that?" I asked, lifting my head up and banging it again, this time against the door frame. I winced, rubbing the back of my head again.

Kenney started laughing, and it was one of those deep belly, hearty laughs. I was beginning to wonder if he was even breathing in between laughter. When he finally stopped laughing, he said, "You know how loud she listens to her music in the car. She'll love it."

"Yeah, you're right." My thoughts trailed off as I began formulating new plans for the car.

"What're you doing this weekend?" Kenney asked, pulling out a cigarette and lighting it, offering me the lighter. I took the lighter, pulling out my own cigarette and lit it.

"I've got a softball game," I said, puffing on the cigarette.

"A softball game? You just hit your head twice within five minutes you clutz."

I couldn't help but laugh. He was right. I was probably one of the clumsiest people in the world. When it came to being on the baseball diamond, however, I somehow managed to stay on my feet. I may not have been the best baseball player, but I certainly wasn't the worst.

"Yeah," I finally said. "Why don't y'all come and watch? You and Maye?"

Kenney took a hit off his cigarette, rubbing his chin. "Yeah, I think we can do that."

Josh and I pulled into the parking lot of the sports complex, unloading our stuff and making our way towards the field. I had new white and blue cleats on my feet, a pair of black baseball pants, and our blue jerseys. Josh wore a similar outfit, but his shoes were all red. We went half and half on a softball bat, figuring we could both use it.

We got to the dugout, unpacking our stuff and getting ready to hit the field. I grabbed my glove and a ball. Josh grabbed his, and we went into the field to start throwing. I rolled my shoulders, loosening them up. I hadn't thrown a ball in a couple of years. I reared back and threw the ball, the ball went flying way too far to the left, completely out of Josh's reach.

"Damn man," Josh said, running to grab the ball rolling across the outfield. "You haven't practiced in a while, have you?"

He threw the ball back from where it had stopped, a perfect line drive straight to my glove. "Nope, but the good news is you don't make many throws on first base."

I threw the ball back to him, not in a straight line but within his reach this time. "I just need to warm up." I shrugged.

Josh reached out to his left, catching the ball in his mitt. "Isn't that Bailey's parents?" Josh asked, nodding his head towards the bleachers.

I turned around to see Kenney and Maye walking toward the bleachers. Maye pulled out her blanket and laid it across the metal, cold from the frigid winter air. I turned back to Josh. "I'll be right back." I took off sprinting to the fence closest to where Kenney and Maye were sitting.

"Thanks for coming, y'all," I said as I reached the fence. I wrapped my fingers in between the chain length fence.

"Hey, sweetie," Maye said, her phone in her hand. "Look who we've got on the phone!" She turned her phone to me to show a live video of Bailey.

"Hey baby!" She shouted from within the phone. "Good luck!"

"Thanks, babe," I smiled, my cheeks flushing red. "Alright, I've got to get back to it." I made my way over to Josh where we continued warming up.

Hours went by as the game went back and forth. It was the top of the last inning, we were down by one and had two outs with nobody on base. I stepped up to the plate. I hadn't got a single hit all night, and it was bringing me down. I was beginning to question the decision to even play. I spread my feet, slightly bending my knees. I rested the bat on my shoulder, waiting for the pitch. I took a deep breath, exhaling the nerves out of my system.

The large yellow ball looked like the sun cutting through the night sky. The ball left his hand, arching and then dropping back down. I leaned on my back foot, lifted my bat off my shoulder, swinging the bat when the ball crossed the plate. The *ping* of the ball leaving the aluminum bat echoed throughout the sports complex, and I took off running.

The ball whistled through the air in a line drive, landing in between the left and center fielders, rolling all the way to the fence. I glanced over to see where the fielders were when I got to second base and decided to take the turn. I rounded the base and heard the other team shouting "Three! Three!"

I dove forward, laying my body on the ground as I slid to the base. I reached out, grabbing the side of the base as the third baseman brought his glove down on my helmet. "Safe!" I heard the umpire call. I jumped up, clapping my hands and looking at my team's dugout. All the men in there were clapping and cheering, it felt good. I heard Bailey screaming from Maye's phone, cheering me on. Even if she couldn't be here in person, she still found a way to support me.

Josh was next up. He readied himself in the box, taking a similar approach to my stance but more straight up and down. "Come on now kid, go yard!" I shouted from third base. He looked over at me, throwing a sly smile my way. He was getting ready to hit a homerun. I knew that look. The pitcher tossed the ball, a lower arc than the one he'd thrown me. It bounced in front of Josh, popping him in the shin.

After he mouthed a few expletives, Josh got back in the box. He was even more fired up now. The pitcher tossed the ball again. It arced up, and then back down. Josh pulled his body weight back, exploding his arms out in front of him as the bat made contact with the ball. The *ping* from his hit echoed throughout the complex, louder than mine had been. The ball soared off his bat, heading straight for the trees on the other side of the outfield fence.

I jumped up, throwing my hands in the air as the ball left the field. I tagged home plate, securing my run, and waited for Josh to come around. When he got there, I slapped his helmet and said, "Now that's what I'm talking about."

The next batter struck out, and we went back into the field. Josh was back on shortstop and I was on first, where we had both been all night. He had been making phenomenal plays all night, reminding me of watching him play growing up. The first two batters up were easy pop fly outs. The final batter got up to the plate. He was one of their power hitters. He cracked his neck as he wiggled the bat around and got into position.

I looked over at Josh, who returned my gaze, smiled then nodded. Josh playfully winked at me, laughing as we turned back around to face the batter. I bent my knees, readying myself for a play. The first pitch he saw, he drilled to shortstop. Josh dove to his left, the ball hitting the inside of his glove. He propped himself up on his knee and whipped the ball across the field. I stretched out, back foot on the bag and front foot as far forward as I could go nearly doing a perfect split. I heard the heavy steps of the runner and I stretched myself as far as I could go.

The ball hit my glove, as I did a full split. My back foot shifted off the bag after I caught it. The runner didn't slow down, running full force towards the bag. When he got closer, his foot stepped on my ankle, laying out beside the bag. I fell back and screamed in pain, reaching down and grabbing my ankle.

Before I knew it, Josh was by my side. "Let me see it, man," he said, lifting my pants leg up. My ankle looked like someone had stuffed the softball in my foot. "Let's get you to the ER, man." Josh wrapped his arm around my shoulder and slowly helped me up to one leg.

Josh looked over at me and I asked, "Was he out?"

Josh laughed. "Your ankle is swollen to the size of an actual softball, and you're worried about the out?"

"Yes, exactly. I don't want this injury to be for nothing." I winced in pain.

"Yes, he was out," Josh laughed again, shaking his head.

As we walked out of the dugout, Kenney and Maye ran up to us. "Josh, where are you taking him? Is it okay if we come?" Maye asked as Kenney came around to the side of me opposite Josh, supporting me with his arm.

"Yeah, of course," Josh said as they helped me hobble to the parking lot. When I got to the car, I carefully slid into the passenger seat, ass first with my legs still extended outside of the car.

Maye walked around to my side of the car, her phone still in her hand. She handed me the phone, revealing Bailey's worry-stricken face still on the screen. "Hey, babe," I said, reaching back and rubbing my neck.

"That looked bad, Clay," she said. "Let me see it."

"It's fine." I pointed the phone's camera down at my swollen ankle. I slid the sock gently off my foot, wincing when I finally pulled it off.

"Baby..." she murmured, looking at my enlarged, black and blue ankle.

I laid back in the hospital bed as the curtains to my little room opened, and Mom came in, dropping her purse in an empty chair and rushing to my side. "Are you okay?"

"I'm fine, just a little sore," I said. I looked around the room at all the people there for me. Josh, Mom, Matt, Kenney, and Maye were all packed in the tiny room I was stashed in. "Y'all really didn't have to come."

"Well, someone had to drive you," Josh joked from the corner, looking up from his phone.

I nodded my head. "True. But seriously, I appreciate all of you being here."

Mom leaned in, kissing the top of my forehead. "Sorry I didn't make the game sweetie. I got caught up at work."

"Mom, it really is fine," I promised, taking her hand in mine. "Have you met Bailey's parents yet?"

"No, I don't think so," she said standing back up and turning to the two people she didn't know in the room.

She extended her hand to Maye first. "I'm Susan Crawford, Clay's mom," she said as Maye took her hand and stood up, pulling her in for a hug.

"Thank you for the way you've raised this boy. Both of your boys are fine young men, and you should be proud," Maye said, letting go of her and leaning back. "I'm Maye Frey, and this is my husband Kenney."

"And this," Mom started, pointing her thumb at Matt, still standing in front of the curtain. "Is my husband Matt." Kenney stood, shaking Mom's hand and then Matt's.

The doctor peeked through the curtains, entering the already crowded room and making his way to the computer at my bedside. He was a younger doctor, probably in his early forties, maybe late thirties. He had jet black slicked back hair, and a clean-shaven face. "Clay, I've got some good news and bad news. Which do you want first?"

"Give it to me straight doc," I said, wanting to get it over with.

"Bad news, you fractured your Tibia," he started, flipping his computer screen around to show me the xray images. "Good news, you won't need any surgery. You'll just need to stay off of it for a few weeks and let it heal on its own."

I groaned. "I'm going to be in a boot, aren't I?"

The doctor laughed, nodding his head. "I take it you've worn one before?"

"Yup," Mom spoke up. "When he fractured his ankle playing ball in high school." Thanks Mom.

"I knew it," Kenney laughed from the corner. All eyes raced over to him. "Clay told me he was going to play, but as clumsy as he is I figured it would be a sight to see. Now that I know you did the same thing when you played before, it just solidifies the fact that you're clumsy as hell."

We couldn't help but laugh because he was right.

It's Going to be a White Trans Am

Fracturing my ankle had really put a cog in the plans of working on the Trans Am for Bailey. Luckily, Kenney was more than willing to help with the stuff he could. I was able to do some things, like changing the taillights and headlights, but Kenney handled the rest of the mechanical work. He pushed himself from underneath the car, standing up and handing me a rag coated in grease.

"Did you get it?" I asked as I slid a cigarette out of his pack and handed it to him.

"I sure as hell hope so. I don't want to go back under there," he said, sticking the cigarette between his lips.

I hobbled off the stool I sat on, making my way to the driver's side. I stuck the key in the ignition and brought the car to life. It roared in the small garage. "Anything?" I yelled over the roar of the engine.

Kenney bent down, looking underneath the car. He finally stood back up. "Nope, nothing. It's not leaking anymore, I think we're good. Kill it." He motioned his hand in front of his neck.

I turned the key, bringing the garage back to silence and hobbled back to my stool. "So," I started, closing the driver's side door. "Mechanically, we're done."

Kenney nodded, taking a seat beside me. "What's next?"

I started looking around the car, pondering what I wanted to do next. "Well," I said, standing up again and hobbling around the car. "I think the stripes are next. I'll call in the morning and get an appointment to have them put on and the new body parts color matched."

"Hey Maye," I spoke into the car speaker when she picked up the phone. "I just left the doctor's office, they cleared me from the boot, everything is healing fine. I need a favor, though."

"Okay, sweetie, I'm listening," she said with a hint of curiosity and worry tainting her tone.

"The car is done, the stripes are on, paint done, dried and ready to go. Would you mind giving me a ride down there in a few? I'll need the spare key. I told them just to lock the key in it.

"Sure, sweetie. Just come by the house and we can head over there."

We said our goodbyes, and I headed to their house. I'm not going to lie; I was a bit worried. I still hadn't got the car inspected and the tags on it were dead, so driving it on the road was always a gamble. It was a chance I had to take.

My phone rang again, Maye's name appeared on my phone. I pressed the button on the steering wheel and answered, "Hello?"

"I'll meet you at the gas station down the road. Bailey's home early for winter break. She'll have all kinds of questions if you show up, and we leave together. She'll probably want to go."

"I'll take the car to Mom's and leave it at her house until I can get it back in the garage without her seeing it then," I said, my gears turning, trying to make sure we didn't get caught. "I'll be there in about ten minutes."

"Sounds good sweetie. I'll see you there." She hung up the phone.

Well, this certainly made things more interesting. Not only was I driving a car with dead tags, but I'd also be avoiding my girlfriend. I was excited that she was home, though, and couldn't wait to see her.

I pulled into the gas station, spotting Maye's car sitting in the back of the parking lot. I pulled up beside her. I jumped out of the car and into Maye's car, buckling my seatbelt. "When did Bailey get here?" I asked as we drove off.

"Like fifteen minutes after you called me. You also aren't supposed to know. She wanted to surprise you, too. So act surprised when you see her," Maye laughed.

When we finally got to the body shop, I spotted the Trans Am sitting out front. It was truly beautiful under the moonlight, the snow-white body shimmering in the stars, the new black stripes running from the hood scoop to the back of the car. The black headlights stared you down like angry eyes. She was going to love it.

Maye handed me the spare key and said, "I'll follow behind you. As long as they can't read your tags, you should be good."

I nodded and smiled, getting out of the car and into the Trans Am. I felt goosebumps line my arms as I got ready to crank the car. It was done, everything on the car was finally fixed. It ran like it should, all the cosmetics were done, it was finally ready for Bailey.

I turned the ignition as the car struggled to turn over. I tilted my head to the side, waiting for some response from the car. Finally, it turned over and the car roared to life. The interior lit up like a rocket ship, the headlights shone bright in front of me. It was ready to drive.

I pulled out of the parking spot, making my way back onto the main road with Maye close behind. I got to the stoplight, preparing to do a u-turn when the car cut off. It didn't sputter, it didn't flicker, it just cut off. I quickly grabbed the key, trying to crank the car again. *Tick, tick, tick* was the only sound the car made.

"Fuck!" I yelled, slamming my fists into the steering wheel. This couldn't be happening. My heart started racing in my chest, beating against my chest cavity like a mad man beating down the doors. My hands went numb as the feeling escaped me. My breathing got heavy, constricting almost. I slumped forward, my head landing on the steering wheel. I was in full blown panic attack mode.

As the shallow light began to disappear from my vision and my head felt like it was swelling to the size of a watermelon, the car door opened, and the sound of the busy road and honking horns filled my ears.

"Clay," Maye said, leaning into the car and rubbing my back. "What happened?"

"I don't know," I groaned, my head still against the steering wheel. "It cut off. It just cut off, and now it won't crank. What if the police come, Maye? I'm screwed. I can't afford a ticket. I don't want to get in trouble. What if they tow the car and I have to pay to get it out?"

"Sweetie, it'll be okay, I promise. Take a deep breath for me, please," she pleaded. I paused my buzzing mind and inhaled a deep breath, taking in the scents of gas and ash around me. I exhaled, letting it all out, trying to force the panic attack out of my system. "There you go," Maye said, continuing to rub my back.

I took another deep breath, opening my eyes as I exhaled. I lifted my head off the steering wheel to thank Maye, but the flashing blue lights in my rearview mirror caught my attention first. Shit. Of course. I saw the officer step out of his car, putting on his poncho as the rain started to fall. Maye threw her hood over her head, stepping out of the way. I got out of the car, turning to face the fast-approaching officer.

"Good evening, I'm officer Mullins with the Myrtle Beach police department. How we doin' tonight folks?" he asked as he got to the car. He walked right past the back of the car and to where Maye and I were standing.

"I've been better," I half-heartedly laughed. "Car cut off and I can't get it to crank. I reckon I'm going to have to call a tow truck."

He stepped back, looking at the car. "Nice ride you got here."

"Thank you sir, it's actually a Christmas present for my girlfrie nd.".

"Well you are a lucky lady," he said, turning to Maye.

Maye burst out laughing. "I'm his girlfriend's mom."

Officer Mullins cheeks lit up, matching the red light shining from the stop light. He rubbed the side of his head and said, "Sorry about that. You look so young ma'am. Look, let's get your car pushed over to that parking lot so you're out of the street while we wait on the tow truck."

We? Was he planning on staying until the tow truck got here? I hoped not, it would just mean more opportunity for him to see the dead tags. "Yeah, that sounds good. Maye, you want to get in and steer while we push?"

"You just got your boot taken off, Clay, are you sure I shouldn't push?" Maye asked.

I shook my head. "No, I need to get used to being on it. Everything's healed." I think.

"Okay, but if it starts to hurt you stop, and we'll switch places." Maye climbed into the driver's seat and shifted the car to neutral. We walked to the back of the car as she yelled back, "Ready when you are!"

Officer Mullins and I stood at the back of the car, pushing it while Maye turned the steering wheel hard. I pushed all of my weight into the car, forcing it forward until we got it into the parking lot.

I could feel the force being put on my ankle, the searing pain coursing through my foot and leg. I continued to push through, standing in the middle of the car. I gritted my teeth together as my nose scrunched up. I kept pushing through the pain.

Once we stopped, I leaned against the car and slumped down to my bottom. I rested my head against the back of the car. Yes, I was exhausted. Yes, I was also trying to cover the tags.

I pulled out my phone, calling the nearest tow truck company. Once I got off the phone, Officer Mullins turned back to me. "Are they on their way?"

"Yes, sir," I nodded.

"Well, if you don't need me for anything else, I'll be on my way."

"No sir, I think we are good. Thank you for your help," I said, sincerity filling my voice.

"Of course." He nodded his head and turned to walk away. He took a couple of steps forward and stopped in place, turning around to face me. "Oh, and get your tags renewed. Merry Christmas."

C hristmas Eve quickly came the week after the car was done. Well, after I finished changing the alternator that had caused it to cut off in the middle of the road. I was so excited to give Bailey her car. The expression on her face was the thing I most anticipated, seeing her eyes light up. At least, that's what I hoped would happen.

I kept the car at Mom's house after getting an inspection and the tags renewed. I kept it back behind everything, the house, the shed, and the barn. It was tucked away so far back that Mom forgot it was even there sometimes.

She wasn't crazy about the idea of me giving Bailey the car for Christmas, and I couldn't say I blamed her. We had been together for six months, but something inside of me just told me this was what I needed to do. Something told me she was different, and she deserved this. That was what I was going with, that strong feeling overwhelming me every time I thought about her.

Some people buy expensive diamond rings at the same price I spent on the car, and nobody bats an eye. The idea of a car seemed like a big one, but I was smart about costs. I nickel and dimed where I could, getting some parts used, doing most of the work with Kenney. So the idea was different, but I think it's more practical than a diamond ring.

I pulled into Mom's driveway off the old dirt road. Bailey was meeting me here for Christmas Eve with Mom, Matt, Josh and my grandparents. As I got out of my car, I saw Bailey's van pull into the driveway. I did a quick check to make sure she couldn't see the Trans Am hidden in the back. Once I confirmed that, I turned to wait for Bailey with a wide smile spread across my face.

Bailey got out of the car, falling into my outstretched arms. I wrapped my arms around her torso, pulling her in close. I leaned down, laying my lips on hers, and igniting the burning passion flowing through us. Every time our lips met, it sent a fire through my body that made me light up like the sun. That feeling alone was worth every minute we spent together.

"Are your grandparents here already?" She asked as she pulled her lips slowly away from mine.

"Yes," I said, nodding.

I took her hand and we walked up Mom's steps and into the house. As soon as the door broke the threshold, Pops came skidding around the corner barking. Once he saw us, though, he stopped barking and started wagging his tail, running to jump up on Bailey and completely bypassing me.

Mom walked around the corner next. "Pops get down, quit it now," she scolded. "Come in you two." We followed behind her, going into the living room where everybody else was.

Ma was the first one to stand up, like always. She walked to us wrapping her arms around Bailey first. "It's so good to see you, sweetie."

Bailey smiled softly, hugging her back. "It's good to see you too! I have missed y'all." Bailey loved my family, and they loved her. They saw her as family, embracing her. They had never acted like this with any other girl, so this was really special to me.

Josh stood up and walked to me, putting his arm around my shoulder, turning me to walk away. "I guess I'll be back Bailey," I laughed.

"We'll make her feel right at home," Mom said, offering Bailey her seat.

Josh and I walked through the house, making our way out the back door. We sat on the steps and I pulled out a cigarette and lit it, putting it to my lips and inhaling the cool menthol flavor.

"What's up, man?" I asked.

"So you really got her a car for Christmas?"

I laughed, "No, I fixed up a car for her for Christmas."

"You think she's worth it?"

"I know she is. The way I feel when I'm around her, how there isn't ever a frown on my face if she's with me. The way I feel when we kiss. It feels like tiny jolts running up and down my body. She makes me happier than I have ever been before," I said, the cigarette burning away in my mouth.

"Look at the way y'all treat her. Ma and Pa love her. Mom treats her like a daughter already. You seem to love her, even Matt talks to her, and he doesn't talk to anyone."

He looked at me, nodding his head. "I can tell. We can all tell, even Ma and Pa were talking about how much happier you've seemed lately. I'm not going to lie. We were getting worried about you. You really fell off the deep end for a bit."

I knew he was right. My senior year of college at Coastal Carolina had been tough. I was overloaded with work, working fifty, sixty, even seventy hours a week at times. My course load was full, so I could graduate on time. I started drinking more, using drugs, spending time away from the family more. I had been going through some dark stages in my life. My mental health had been the worst. That had all changed when I met Bailey.

"I'm sorry."

"Hey," he said, wrapping his arm around me. "Don't be sorry. We understood what you were going through. We just wanted you to be okay."

"It's still early, but she might be the one."

Josh cut his eyes over at me, wide with surprise. "Really?"

"I love her more than I've ever loved a girl before. I can't see myself without her now, and I don't want to."

Josh moved his hand to my right shoulder, lifting himself off the steps. I followed suit, putting my cigarette out in the nearby ashtray. "I'm glad you're happy," Josh finally said. We made our way back inside to hear the sound of laughter and happiness emitting from the living room. My family loved her just as much as I did, and that made me all the surer about my feelings.

Christmas finally came and my nerves were through the roof. I was so worried it would scare her away going this big, but I also thought she would love it. Honestly, I didn't know what to think because I had never done something this big before. I just wanted to show her I loved her in every possible way.

I stayed at Mom's that Christmas Eve, so I would be able to spend more time with my family, especially after the conversation Josh and I'd had. Bailey had stayed for a long time the night before, eating Christmas Eve dinner and drinking eggnog with us. However, when she left I ran out back to move the car to the front.

I was going to drive the car there, while her parents kept her occupied and inside. I bought her two smaller gifts as a joke, one was a muscle car calendar and the other was a toy Trans Am. I wanted to drop subtle hints to her to see if she caught on.

I slid into the driver's seat of the Trans Am, bringing the roaring engine to life. The sound of the engine rumbling filled the air, roaring as it idled down. I took off towards Bailey's house with the car. The closer I got, the more my heart beat against my chest. It felt like I was having a heart attack. The anxiety flooded my mind again, making me question everything.

My foot slowly pushed the gas pedal down further as the anticipation in my mind swarmed around. I gripped the steering wheel with all the strength in my hands, squeezing the color out of my own hands. My vision started to glaze over, and I shook my head, trying to pull myself out of it.

I took several deep breaths, focusing on the happiness I hoped Bailey would feel when she saw the gift. Calming down, I decided to really put the car to the test. I stomped down on the gas, the engine getting louder as the speed picked up. I knew these backroads like the back of my hand, so I felt comfortable.

45 mph.

55 mph.

65 mph.

75 mph.

85 mph.

I finally let off the gas, the car slowing back down and the sound of the engine dying down. Well, at least I knew it would run at high speeds and not cut off. In fact, the car had given me no problems since I'd changed the alternator. Happiness and calmness finally filled me, and just in time as I pulled into Kenney and Maye's driveway.

I pulled the car into the back yard to keep it hidden. Before the car could come to a complete halt, I was already putting it in park and jumping out of the car, headed for the front door. I leaped up the steps, coming down on my bad ankle. I couldn't hold my weight up as my knee came forward and slammed into the steps.

"Shit," I said, grabbing my ankle and rolling it around. Once the pain subsided, I got to the front door and walked in. I had been over there so much that Kenney and Maye told me to stop knocking and just come in when I got there, so that's what I did. I had the two wrapped joke gifts tucked under my arm when I saw Bailey sitting in her room.

Kenney and Maye looked at me from the kitchen, smiling and waving, nodding their heads towards Bailey's room. Maye looked at me and mouthed, "We will get set up."

I knocked on Bailey's open door, leaning my body against the doorframe and looking in. Bailey sat on her bed and glanced from her phone when she heard the knock. Her face lit up, and I put the gifts on her dresser. I walked over to her, and she leaned her face against my stomach, wrapping her arms around me. I reached down with my arms, returning the hug.

I lifted her chin up with my index finger, facing her eyes and mouth towards me. I leaned in, my lips touching hers. She took my upper lip in between hers, lightly nibbling on it. We continued kissing, our lips doing a magical dance with one another, sliding from side to side. She pulled back slightly, resting her head on mine.

"Here," she said, turning around and grabbing a wrapped gift. It was thin and rectangular, I racked my brain to think of what it could be but came up with nothing.

I sat down and took the perfectly wrapped gift from her hands and began unwrapping it. The wrapping was so perfect, I had to take my time to make sure I didn't just disregard the work she'd put into it. I opened one side, then another, splitting the tape holding it together, and unwrapping it like a deli sandwich.

Sitting in my lap was a black picture frame with "Love, the key that unlocks the heart" written in cursive along the bottom and a picture of Bailey and me from the first wedding we'd attended together. A tear slipped from my eye as I looked up to her and smiled.

"It's perfect," I said, pulling her in for a hug. She nuzzled her head into my arm, embracing my warmth. "Here." I reached for the two embarrassingly badly wrapped gifts and gave them to Bailey. "These are for you." She took the gifts, trying to carefully open the gifts.

"Just rip it off," I laughed.

"Okay," she huffed and began tearing away at the paper. Once she opened the calendar, a look of confusion flooded her face. Just the reaction I expected. She opened the toy car and looked even more confused. "Thank you so much, Clay, I love it," she lied.

I held back a laugh. I appreciated her trying to make me feel better, but I would have to tell her later she didn't have to do that. "I'm glad you like it, baby," I said, standing up. "Come on, let's go outside with everyone. I think all the kids are playing on the trampoline."

When we got to the back door, Kenney came in and stopped us. "Nope," he pulled out a blindfold and wrapped it around Bailey's eyes. "We have another surprise for you." He looked over at me and winked. "Clay, you take her other arm and help me guide her down the ramp." I linked my arm through Bailey's, guiding her out the door and down the ramp on the back porch. Kenney and Maye had gotten a giant bow and put it on the hood of the car.

"Where are we going?" Bailey asked.

"You'll see, be patient," Kenney said.

Once we got closer, Kenney stopped. He looked at me, silently asking me if I was ready. I nodded my head, sucking in a deep breath of air and slowly exhaling. Kenney untied the blindfold, letting it fall to the ground. She stood there, her eyes nearly bulging out of her head.

"I..." she started. "I... Who?"

"Clay." Kenney nudged me.

She whipped her head around facing me, "No you did not." Was she mad? Happy? Upset? Shocked? I couldn't tell.

"I did, babe. You deserved this. I wanted to make sure you had something safe to drive up there. We all know the van wasn't going to make it much longer."

She threw herself into me, laying the side of her face against my chest. She wrapped her arms around me, just under my arms and squeezed. I leaned down, kissing the top of her head and draping my arms over her shoulders. "I love you, Clay Dabrowski. This is the best Christmas present ever. And *you* are the best boyfriend ever."

I smiled into her hair, the cool air nipping at my bare arms. I heard the crackling of the fire pit in the background, listening to Bailey's quiet breaths as I held onto her.

"Let's eat!" Kenney said, clapping his hands together as the smell of the ham and turkey filled everyone's nose.

New Year, Same Me

This New Year's would be the first one I spent with Bailey, and I wanted to make sure we got to kiss when the clock struck midnight. During the Renaissance era, when masquerade balls were common, attendees would remove their masks at midnight to kiss their lover as a way to purify each other from evil and start over with a clean slate. Then English and German folklore expanded on this idea, creating the idea that a midnight kiss strengthens the roots of a growing relationship.

The truth was I had never spent New Year's Eve with a girl, not even back in high school. So, I guess it was fitting the girl I loved more than anybody in the past would be the one with whom I first get to spend New Year's Eve. I knew we needed to make plans, so I took out my phone and called Bailey.

"Hello, handsome," Her voice sang through the other end of the phone.

"Hey you." I smiled at the way her voice brightened up my day. "Do you have plans for New Year's Eve?"

"Your ears must be itching," she laughed. "I was just talking about asking you to come to one of the clubs in Spartanburg. I'm thinking it'll be us, Mary and the guy she's talking to, and some of the other soccer girls."

"Of course. I'm so excited to spend New Year's Eve with you," I said, beaming with excitement.

"Good! Mary wants you to come to meet her new guy, too. She really is starting to think a lot of you."

"That was my goal from the beginning. I wanted to be an extra friend, not steal her friend. I think I'm doing a pretty good job of it."

"You definitely are. I'll see you this weekend, babe. I love you."

"And I love you," I said back, hanging up the phone. I was nervous. I hadn't gone to a club or gone out to socially drink like that with Bailey yet, so who's to say she wouldn't hate drunk me? What if I made an ass out of myself? Maybe I just won't drink. No, I'll drink in moderation.

"Clay!" Mary shouted as I walked through their dorm room door behind Bailey. "Here!" she shoved a bottle of Mad

Dog into my chest. There was going to be no drinking in moderation with Mary.

"I'm good," I laughed, trying to pass the bottle back to her.

She stuck her bottom lip out and rolled her eyes up at me. "I thought you were fun. I guess you just can't drink like me."

"I'm the only one who's even twenty-one here. I think I can handle my own."

"And you think that matters?" Mary said, reaching into her back pocket and pulling out an ID stating she was twenty-three. "I'll outdrink you any and every day."

"You two are about to do it, aren't you?" Bailey asked, shaking her head and stifling a laugh.

"Whoever passes out first loses. Winner gets bragging rights and twenty bucks," Mary said, ignoring Bailey.

"You got yourself a deal," I smiled.

See, before I met Bailey I was big on partying. I was going out almost every night, and the nights that I didn't go out, I was at home drinking. I had been like that since I graduated high school. I felt sheltered when I graduated because I had never smoked, drank, cussed, or even had sex. I was an innocent kid. That was boring.

Mary mulled it over for a minute before saying, "Deal!"

I reached out my hand.

She offered hers, and we shook on it. "So," I said, letting go of her hand. "About this guy."

"Johnny! You're going to love him. He's a baseball player, too," Mary said, excitement lighting up her face. This was the first time I was meeting a guy she talked to, so I assumed it was pretty serious. I was excited to meet him.

A knock came at the door, causing Mary to jump out of bed and run to the door, nearly falling over a pile of clothes in front of her bed. She opened the door and threw her arms around the person on the other side.

"Clay, this is Johnny," Mary said, leading him in by the hand. "Johnny, this is Clay. Bailey's boyfriend."

The guy standing in front of me was an inch or two shorter than me. He had dark skin, accented by a faded haircut. His dark eyes stared a whole through me. Something about him, though, just didn't sit right with me. I got a bad vibe from him, and I didn't like it. I put that feeling aside for Mary and extended my hand to him.

"Nice to meet you, man," I said to him, my hand floating in the air between us.

"You, too," he said stoically, without reaching for my hand. He turned to Mary "When are we leaving?" Yeah, I didn't like him at all.

"We're pregaming here," I said, grabbing another bottle of Mad Dog and handing it to him. "Drink up."

He pushed the bottle away. "Nah, I'm good."

"Oh, lighten up," Mary said, playfully tapping his arm. "He's just nervous, you guys."

Nervous? More like an ass. I extended the bottle back to him. "It's rude to say no the second time," I said half serious and half-jokingly.

He stared down at the bottle, then back at me. He caught my gaze and tried to stare me down as long as he could before blinking. I pushed the bottle further out, nodding it at him.

"Fine," he said, snatching the bottle from me and opening it. He took a small swig before capping it and putting it on the desk behind him.

"Clay and I have a bet," Mary said to him. "Whoever lasts the longest wins bragging rights and a hundred bucks..."

"Whoa," I said, halting her mid-sentence. "We said twenty bucks."

"Oh come on moneybags, you can afford a hundo." I hated when she called me moneybags. Everybody had this notion I was rich or something, but I wasn't. I was just smart with my money and had been saving for a long time.

I scrunched up my nose and huffed. "It's not me I'm worried about."

She rolled her eyes and turned back to Johnny. "Want to join in?"

"No, I'm good," he said, giving a sharp look over to Mary. "I'm going to go smoke."

"Cool, I'll go with you," I said hopping up. He rolled his eyes and turned to the door, and I followed him out. After we got outside and lit our cigarettes, I said, "So what do you think of Mary?"

"She's cool."

"Like, cool as in a fling or cool as in you can see being with her for a bit."

"Does it matter? I'm here, aren't I?"

Who the hell did this guy think he was? "It matters to me, because Mary deserves respect."

"Don't tell me what my girl deserves. You worry about your own." He turned to me. I was not a fan of this guy already, what did Mary even see in him?

"Look man, Mary is my friend and I only have her best interest at heart," I said, irritation blatant in my tone.

"Yeah, that needs to stop."

I arched my eyebrows, stunned. "Excuse me?"

"You two don't need to be so close, so back down," he said, flicking an ember off his cigarette."I'll tell you what..." I threw my cigarette down and stomped on it. "Go fuck yourself." I walked back to the room, biting my tongue. Tonight wasn't the night to start something, and I wasn't going to ruin Mary's New Year's Eve celebration.

I stood outside the door, closing my eyes and taking a deep breath to try and calm myself down. I didn't want to give Mary or Bailey any indication of what had just happened. I figured Johnny didn't care enough to say anything either.

I let out one final exhale as I entered the room. Mary shoved another drink in my face as I crossed the threshold, and I couldn't help but to laugh. Despite Johnny, it was going to be a good night.

The bartender sat down the fourth shot of Tequila in front of Mary and me. I picked mine up, looking over at Mary. "Sure you want to keep going?"

"Look," she started, blinking rapidly a couple of times. "This is only the fourth one."

"Yeah, the fourth shot of tequila, tenth shot of the night. You're looking a little wasted," I joked, teasing her. She took the shot glass, throwing it back as the liquid burned down her throat and into her stomach. She slammed the glass down on the bar top, looking over at me.

"You're up, champ," she said, a hiccup ending her sentence for her.

I rolled my shoulders dramatically, cracked my neck, and grabbed the shot glass. "To our *friendship*," I said, emphasizing friendship in front of Johnny. I threw the shot back, feeling the burn crawl down my throat, and drip into my stomach. "Ahhhh." I sighed, setting the glass down.

"Time to dance!" Mary yelled, twirling around in the barstool and hoping off, headed towards the dance floor.

I got up and extended my hand to Bailey. "Care for a dance?"

She laughed, getting out of her seat and taking my hand. "Do you know how to dance, sir?"

"Nope," I led her to the dance floor. "You're going to dance, and I'm going to stand there awkwardly."

"Is that so?"

I stopped on the dance floor, twirling around to face her. I spun her around, pulling her body into me. I grabbed her waist and whispered into her ear, "Dance for me." I lightly bit her ear before moving my face away.

I could see the corners of her mouth turn up as she bit the corner of her lip. She wrapped one hand around my head, moving her body up and down mine, side to side. She slithered down, her ass touching my knees, and then pushed her way back up. She turned her head to the side, and I leaned in to plant a kiss on her lips.

She ran her body up and down mine as the beat of the club music blared, silencing the voices of the club goers. It was crowded on the dance floor and the temperature rose. Sweat beaded on my head, dripping down to my neck. Bailey's red hair started to turn stringy from the heat.

The music came to an end and we made our way off the dance floor. "I'll be right back," I said to Bailey, letting go of her hand. "I've got to use the bathroom."

"Hurry, it's almost midnight! And I expect a kiss."

I smiled at her and blew her a kiss before making my way to the back of the club.

I stood at the urinal, my hand braced against the sticky wall to keep myself from swaying. I did not intend to get this drunk, but here I was. Bailey was perfect, spending New Year's Eve with her was perfect.

I zipped up my pants, walking out of the bathroom. Across the dance floor, I could see Bailey standing against the wall and I made my way to her. As I got closer, a guy stepped up to her, a drink in his hand. He turned slightly, pouring something in the drink.

The closer I got, I could hear their conversation.

"Hey girl, want a drink?" He asked, extending a clear cup full of liquor to her.

Bailey shook her head, pushing the drink away. "I'm good. I'm just waiting on my boyfriend."

"Well, I don't see him here now, why can't I talk to you?"

"Because I'm right here mother fucker," I said, stepping up beside him. I was still pissed from the confrontation with Johnny earlier and the alcohol didn't exactly help. It wasn't a good combination with the medicine I was on. "Do we have a problem?"

He looked over at me, pulling his head back as he swayed in his spot. I think he was more drunk than I was. "Nah man, I was just offering her a drink."

"And did she see the bartender pour that drink?" I asked, already knowing the answer.

"I brought it to her," he said, a slight hiccup following.

I slapped the cup out of his hand, pushing him to the wall with my arm across his neck. "Disgusting. Preying on innocent girls. I saw you pour something in that drink."

"Nah, man," he squeaked. "I didn't do that."

I pushed my arm harder into his throat and I whispered into his ear, "Get out of here." I stepped back, removing my arm from his throat as he made a speedy exit.

I turned back to Bailey, wrapping her in my arms. "I shouldn't have left you alone," I said into her ear.

She wrapped her arms around me, sliding her hands up my back to my shoulders. "I'm glad you saw him do that. I wouldn't have taken it, but some other girl might have."

"I can't stand people like that," I sighed.

Mary and Johnny walked up to us, wide-eyed. "What the hell just happened?" Mary asked, staring at me.

"He poured something in a drink and offered it to Bailey. Then lied to my face about it. So," I started, turning my eyes to Johnny. "I wanted to make sure he didn't do that to anyone else, and he needed to be taught a lesson. He's lucky it wasn't worse."

Johnny chuckled a little bit, pursing his lips and raising his eyebrows. "I'm sure, buddy."

Mary reached over and slapped his arm. I laughed, shaking my head. "Little known fact, I wrestled from middle to high school. So yeah, I think I could have taught the drunk son of a bitch a lesson. Just like I would with anybody who tries to mess with the people I care about."

The music died down as the TVs around the club lit up with a scene from New York. The countdown had begun and taken over where the music left off. As the count got to ten, everyone started cheering along.

"Five...

Four...

Three...

Two...

One...

HAPPY NEW YEAR!" I took Bailey in my arms, pulling her into my body as my lips touched hers. I ran my hand up and down her back, her hands cupped around my face. I embraced her lips, taking them in between my teeth as I pulled back. I rested my head against hers as her eyes fluttered open and we stared deep into one another's souls.

The next day as I was headed back home from Spartanburg, Kenney called me. "Hello?" I answered.

"Where are you at?" His question was blunt, no emotion attached to it. It was almost a statement, as if he knew where I was.

"Headed back to Myrtle."

"From where?" Now irritation seeped through his voice. He knew. Why was he asking me? Was he trying to catch me in an 'ah-ha' moment?

"Spartanburg."

"Yeah," he scoffed. "That's what I figured. Bailey always spends New Year's Eve with us. So she bailed on us for you. Got it."

"That's not what happened Kenney..."

"Save it." He hung up the phone. The silence lingered, the only noise was the roar of the engine of my Challenger. I stared blankly ahead at the road, my mind racing. Why was he mad at me? I wasn't trying to steal Bailey away. I wanted to be part of the family not tear it apart.

Anxiety

I struggle with depression, anxiety, and bipolar. It's a constant battle every day to see life is worth fighting for. You see, it's hard to focus on the good things with anxiety. Your mind is constantly going to the worst possible situations. That overwhelming sensation kicks your depression into high gear because you always worry you're going to screw up.

Alas, the bipolar takes the reins and thrusts you into a manic state. Everything seems good. You're getting the things you want, going out with friends, loving life. But then anxiety takes over and you check your bank account and think about how much money you spent. Another overwhelming sensation takes over and the depression surrounds you. Am I going to have enough money for bills?

It's a never-ending cycle. Living through that constantly is hard. I've worked to find a right medicine combination, and some work better than others.

It was a trial-and-error search for the combination that made the anxiety less overwhelming, the depression much more tolerable and shorter, and the bipolar episodes come further apart. At least, that's the goal.

But Bailey. She just worked for me. She had done more for me than any of the medicine. In her presence, everything felt okay. There was no worry in my life. I knew everything would be okay as long as we were together.

The depression was nonexistent with her. Never a sad moment if I was with her. At least not one that would spiral me into oblivion. She made me happy, carefree. She brought out the me that I had hidden away for so long.

It made the bipolar episodes easier to handle. Not many people knew about my diagnosis because it was a less than favorable diagnosis. People often equate bipolar to crazy, dangerous, and violent. And that's so far from the truth it wasn't even funny.

But the honeymoon phase was over. The anxiety eventually reared its ugly head and took over. It manifested in the form of jealousy this time. The pain from my previous relationship made an appearance. I started trying to poke apart our relationship, so I wouldn't get hurt again.

It started one night when she told me she was going out clubbing with her friends. She had done it plenty of times before. Thirsty Thursday. I remember my college days. Who am I to try and stop that? I would never tell her what she could and couldn't do. She was a grown woman capable of making her own decisions.

But this particular night I thought to myself, 'hm, what if she's not going with her friends but another guy?' That was it. There went the trigger that set off the chain reaction. I started anxiously checking my phone, waiting for her messages. As the night went on, the text messages came further apart, like they normally did.

I got jealous. That was it. She was cheating on me, and I knew it. I tried calling her. She didn't answer. I sent her a final text for the night.

"Bailey, I really do love you. I'm sorry I'm not enough for you, I hope I can earn you back. I want to be able to take you in my arms all the time, and it kills me to know I can't. I'm going to bed. I'll talk to you tomorrow."

I laid my phone down on the side table beside my futon bed. I closed my eyes, taking in a deep breath and letting my mind rest. As I started to doze off, my phone rang. My eyes shot open, and I rolled over.

Bailey's name flashed across the screen along with the picture of us from our first date. I answered the phone. "Hello?"

"Hey, what's going on?" Bailey asked through the phone, worry plaguing her voice. She was genuinely concerned. She had taken time away from her night to call me.

Now I felt bad. "I... I don't know. I just... I got jealous I guess." There it was—my confession.

"Clay..." she whispered, followed by an awkward silence.

"Bailey, go enjoy your night. I'll explain everything tomorrow." I didn't want to take any more time from her night, I felt bad enough.

"Yeah, I think there are some things we need to talk about. We'll talk tomorrow. Get some sleep Clay. I love you."

The next morning, I awakened early. I was nervous. I needed to talk to Bailey, and I knew I did but it didn't make me any less nervous.

I sat anxiously in bed, scrolling through social media. I checked my messages every few minutes, hoping to see a simple 'hey' from her. I wanted nothing more than to apologize, to explain it wasn't her that I didn't trust. Truth be told, I didn't trust myself. I didn't feel like I was good enough to deserve her, or anyone really, but especially her.

My phone buzzed with a text from Bailey. My heart skipped a few beats when I saw her name, and my stomach dropped as the anxiety hit. What if this was it? What if she were done with me after this? I mean I wouldn't blame her. She gave me no reason not to trust her, and yet I still let my emotions override my sensibility.

I picked up the phone, dialing her number.

"Hey there, handsome," she answered.

"Hey babe, how did you sleep?" I asked, the anticipation for our upcoming conversation boiling over the edge.

"I passed out as soon as we got home," she laughed. I loved her laugh, the sound of it made me smile every time. The sweet sound of her laughter was one of my favorite sounds.

"Bailey, I'm sorry," I sighed into the phone. "I made a mistake last night. I let my emotions get the best of me. I let my past catch up to me."

"Clay, it's okay. But I need you to talk to me about these things." The way she cared made me smile, despite the tough conversation. I could tell from her voice she was genuine. She wanted to know my past in order to help my future.

"I know. I knew that last night. I just... wasn't thinking straight. I don't trust easy. I've been cheated on four, five times in every relationship I've been in. After a while, you stop blaming other people and start blaming yourself. What's wrong with me? Was I not enough? It really eats away at you."

"Oh, Clay," she said, sadness in her voice as it flitted away. "You didn't deserve that. Any of it. I wish you would have told me you were having these feelings sooner. We could have worked through it. We still can, Clay. I'm not letting go of you that easy. I will always fight for you and with you, but never against you."

A tear threatened to escape my eye. I bit the bottom of my lip, mulling over what Bailey had just said. She was everything I had ever wanted. So what was holding me back?

"Thank you, Bailey," I finally mustered, wiping away stray tears. "I just... want to give you all of me, but my past holds me back."

"We'll get through it. Together," I heard the confidence radiating in her voice. She cared about me. "I don't know what it feels like, Clay, but I know you don't deserve what they did to you. I will always make sure you don't feel that way with me."

"I can't tell you how much that means to me, Bailey," my voice barely above a whisper. I wanted her to be on this side of the phone with me so bad. I wanted to take her in my arms and hold her close to me. To whisper quiet thank yous into the top of her head. I craved her touch; it made me feel whole.

The following weekend, I decided to make a surprise visit to see Bailey. I wanted to make up for my little fit, and honestly I just wanted to be able to hold her.

I pulled up to the soccer field where the team was practicing. I spotted Bailey's red hair flowing in the wind as she ran down the field dribbling the ball in between her feet. I parked the car facing the field and got out to sit on the hood.

I hopped onto the hood with a solid thud and leaned back, resting my hands behind me as I watched the field. My attention followed Bailey the whole time, watching as her feet worked magic along the field. She was truly special and amazing at everything she did.

Finally, her eyes wandered to mine. A bright, beaming smile crossed her face as she started waving at me. I smiled, chuckling to myself as I waved back to her. She turned and took off towards the opposite end of the field.

My phone buzzed with a message from Kenney. *"Where are you?"* it read.

"Up at Converse. I came to surprise Bailey." I sent back. Suddenly my heart started to beat against my chest. I don't know why I felt so nervous, but I had a bad feeling. Actually, I knew exactly why once I thought about it. He had been cold towards me lately, not saying much to me when I saw him.

"This is the third weekend you've been up there this month. Don't you think that's a little much?" He was mad at me for being up here too much? My heart beat a hammering sound in my ears as my phone shook in my hand.

"It's been a rough month for both of us. She's been studying when I'm here, and I'm helping her." I flipped my phone down on my thigh, leaning my head back and sighing into the sky.

"You okay there, handsome?" I heard Bailey call.

I leaned my head forward, seeing her beauty radiate closer to me. Sure, she had small beads of sweat beating down her face, minimal make up, and her hair was stringy, but she was just as beautiful as ever. To me, it was a different kind of beauty. It was a beautiful display of her passion, of how much she loved the sport and the team. Maybe it was only beautiful to me, and that was okay.

"I am now." I slid off the hood of the car, throwing my arms open as she got closer. She dropped her bag to the ground and wrapped her arms around me.

"I didn't know you were coming, Clay," Bailey said, turning her head up and looking into my eyes. I couldn't tell if she was happy or not, and it kind of concerned me.

"Well, I wanted to make up for what happened the other night. So I figured I could come up to surprise you, and we could just spend time together and talk." I pressed my lips against the top of her head, the tip of my nose lingering above her head as I took in her scent.

She nuzzled her head into my chest. "You didn't have to do that."

I shrugged. "I didn't have to, but I wanted to. I never want you to forget that I love you, and I will work every day to make sure you know it."

She squeezed me a little bit tighter, and I returned the favor. We sat there for a few minutes, holding onto each other and just enjoying one another's touch. My phone buzzed on the hood of the car and we released our grips.

I reached over and checked my phone. *"K."* Yup. Kenney was mad.

We laid in bed later that night, both playing games on our phone. This wasn't what I wanted to come up here for, but she had kind of shut me out. I chalked it up to her being tired from practice, but of course my mind had other ideas.

"Are you mad at me still?" I asked, rolling over to face her, propped up on my elbow.

She gave me an odd look over her phone, cocking her head to the side and quirked her eyebrow. "When was I even mad at you?"

She didn't remember. She's not mad. Or she wanted me to say what I had done wrong. "For the other night, getting so jealous."

"Clay," she started. "I was never mad at you. I was concerned, but not mad."

I sighed, my gaze leaving hers and dropping down to the sheets. I felt like I had let her down. I glanced back up at her. "I'm sorry." Was all I could think to say.

Bailey cocked her head slightly, eyeing me a bit. "For what, Clay?"

"Being like this." I buried my face into my hands and clenched my jaw.

Bailey reached over, slowly rubbing the side of my arm. She lowered her head to be eye level with me. "Look at me," she whispered.

Hesitantly, I brought my gaze to meet hers. She stared at me with those eyes that just read right through me. Her eyes flickered back and forth. "Don't ever apologize to me for being you. I love you for who you are Clay."

"My girlfriend in high school preferred to give me the silent treatment than to talk things out. I always knew she was mad at me because she would go days without talking to me. It was like I didn't exist to her until it was convenient. I'm just kind of stuck with this notion that that's how every girl treats me."

"Clay, I would never do that to you. You deserve better. You deserve love and respect. You deserve people trying just as hard as you. You deserve the best."

I tried to figure out what to say next. What was there to say? "You mean it?" Clever.

"I mean it." She leaned in, pressing her nose against mine, our foreheads slowly coming together. I closed my eyes again, searching my memory for a time when I'd been this comfortable with someone. When someone had felt how Bailey felts about me. And honestly, there was no one.

I reached in, gently swaying my lips across hers. Her eyes fluttered closed, and she returned the kiss. I took her lip in between mine, as I slowly pulled away. "Thank you, Bailey. For being mine and letting me be yours."

As the weeks passed, things were getting easier for me the more comfortable I got with Bailey. I stopped being jealous for no reason. I took what Bailey said and used it as my motivation. To be better, to love myself more.

But I loved her now. With Valentine's Day coming up and on a weekend, Bailey would be home. The pressure was on. I scrambled last minute to come up with an idea I felt worthy of being Bailey and mine's first Valentine's Day. Dinner and a movie was too cliche and boring. I wanted to really wow her.

So Bailey being an adrenaline junkie like myself, I decided that we'd go to a zipline park in a swamp. Yes, the ziplines go over the swamp filled with alligators. Talk about thrill seekers.

I wanted to really show Bailey how much she meant to me. I wanted to show her how well I knew her, how much she loved adrenaline rushes. It was little things I hoped would go a long way.

When Valentine's Day came around, everything had been taken care of. And the best part was I'd successfully kept Bailey in the dark. I wanted to surprise her with everything.

I pulled up to her parents' house first thing that morning, the air still chilly and icy dew fresh on the ground. Maye knew everything going on today, and she was surprisingly good at keeping it from Bailey.

I knocked on the front door, pulling both of my hands up to my mouth and gently blowing on them. I rubbed my knuckles together as Maye opened the door. "What are you waiting for? Get in here," she said, swaying her hand inside.

I stepped by her, noticing Kenney standing in the corner, his arms crossed as he glared at me. Something was off with him still. I hadn't mentioned anything to Bailey because I didn't want to worry her. I kept hoping that things would just get better, or maybe I was overreacting.

I watched Bailey walk out of her room in a pair of khaki pants and a green tank top. Her hair was pulled back in a ponytail. Her minimal makeup highlighted her eyes.

"Hello, beautiful," I smiled.

A grin forced her lips up as she bashfully looked down. "Hello, handsome," she said, lifting her head back up.

I held my arms out and she walked to me, falling into my chest. I wrapped my arms around her and pulled her in. Resting my lips on her head. "Happy Valentine's Day, Bailey."

She lifted her head, looking into my eyes. I loved her gaze, it made me feel at ease. "Happy Valentine's Day, Clay."

"Alright," I said, letting go of her and clapping my hands together. "We have a big day ahead of us, and we've got a reservation to make."

"What could you possibly have reservations for this early, Clay?"

"Ah that's for me to know, and you to find out." I smiled mischievously at her, wiggling my eyebrows playfully.

"Fineeee," she moaned, rolling her eyes and smiling at me. "I guess I'll go." Her grin widened.

I reached my hand out, extending it to her. "Shall we go?"

She reached out, resting her fingers on my palm. "We shall."

The whole ride there she pestered me about where we were going, poking at my ribs and making me jump in my seat. Once we finally got there though, her jaw dropped.

"Best Valentine's Day date ever!"

I chuckled as I put the car in park. I glanced over at her, leaning in to kiss her. My lips met hers, and I felt a warming sensation run through my body. I pulled back, smiling at her softly.

I got out of the car, rushing around the back of the car to get to Bailey's door. I grabbed the door handle, opening the door for Bailey and swaying my arm outward. "After you my love."

Bailey giggled, looking up at me with a smile. "You're something else, Clay Dabrowski."

I cocked my head to the side and shot my eyebrows up. "But you wouldn't have me any other way?"

She got out of the car, bringing her body to mine. "I wouldn't have you any other way," she whispered into my ear. She walked away from the car with a slight laugh. She knew what she was doing, clever girl.

I tailed behind her, half jogging to catch up. Once I got to her, I wrapped my arms around her waist and pulled her into me, kissing the side of her cheek. "You're going to love this."

"I've always wondered about this place. Is it really ziplining over a swamp?" She asked, nearly bouncing out of her shoes.

I smiled, turning towards her and watching the child like enjoyment building in her eyes. This is what I wanted. It was all I needed, to see her happy, to be the source of this happiness. "Yes, ziplining over the swamp," I chuckled as we made our way to the entryway.

"Welcome to Swamprat's Zip Line!" The short, young girl standing at the front desk chirped as we entered. Her short blonde hair curled so tight it bounced when she spoke. "Do y'all have reservations?"

I walked to the counter, Bailey following closely behind me. I had her fingers wrapped gently in my hand. "Two for Dabrowski."

"Ah yes, the intermediate course. That's the one with the most gators," she winked as she chuckled. "Your total will be $54.95." I paid for the reservations and made our way to the waiting room.

After a few minutes, a college-aged woman and a middle-aged woman came in. The older woman was about the same size as the girl at the front desk, with long black hair tied in a ponytail. The younger girl was much taller than the girl at the front desk. Her dark brown hair draped across her shoulders. "We ready?"

Bailey hopped up from her seat, pulling me up with her. "Oh yes! This is going to be so much fun."

As they led us outside, she chuckled. "First time?"

"Yeah, best way to spend Valentine's Day," Bailey said, turning her head to me. She squeezed my hand and smiled her beautiful smile, her shiny white teeth showing.

"Smart man," the college aged woman said. "My name is Kelsey. I'll be your guide today. This is my co-guide Rebecca We'll go through fifteen separate lines today. They'll start off shorter and slower and gradually get longer and faster. Rebecca will zip line down first and be at the next platform to help you.

"First we need to practice on our practice course. We need you to be prepared. It is a dangerous adventure if you don't know what you're doing. We'll practice slowing down and proper riding skills.

"For your equipment, these are your gloves. They are what you'll use to slow yourself down. It prevents your hands from being pinched, or slashed, by the pulley and burned by the rope. Next is your harness. You'll use this to connect to the zipline, obviously so you don't fall into the swamp and get eaten by gators. And your final piece of equipment is your helmet, to protect your head from any kind of injury. Any questions?"

I looked over at Bailey. She was beaming. She seemed so happy to be here, to be spending Valentine's Day with me. That's all I wanted was for her to be happy. To be happy with me. I flashed a smile r when she glanced at me and turned back to Kelsey. "I think we're good."

"Great." She clapped her hands together. "Then we can practice and hit the ropes. We'll let the lady go first. What is your name, ma'am?"

"Bailey," she said as her eyes lit up in excitement.

"Alright, Bailey, here is your equipment," Kelsey handed her a harness, glove, and helmet. "Get everything on and stand on the block over there." She pointed off to the side where Rebecca stood next to the start of a mini zipline. The zipline was only about ten feet off the ground and probably ten feet long.

Bailey quickly slipped on her equipment, sliding her arms through the harness as I held it in place for her, strapping the helmet to her head, and sliding her gloves over her bare hands. She headed to the box and hopped on it. "I'm ready!"

Rebecca walked up to the box, strapping her to the pulley and giving her directions. "Okay, put your left hand on the top of the pulley system and keep your right hand around the rope in front of the pulley. To slow down, you're going to move your right hand in a flat position behind the pulley."

Bailey nodded, you could see the anticipation building up in her. She bounced on the heels of her feet never losing her beautiful smile. She lifted her feet off the box as she began to ride down the zipline. Her eyes lit up, a new burst of excitement filled them as they twinkled. As she got to the end, she moved her hand behind the pulley and slowed herself down to a stop right before the box.

"Ah yes, that brings up a good point. If you stop too soon, I can reel you the rest of the way, however it isn't nearly as fun as riding it the whole way. I will be there to give you guidance on when to start braking," Rebecca said as she unhooked Bailey from the zipline.

After I had my turn on the practice line, Kelsey and Rebecca led us down a trail through the woods. Hand-in-hand, Bailey and I walked, taking in the scenery around us. Around every curve of the path was another breathtaking view of the forest, sometimes with wildlife in sight.

We finally made it to the first platform. Rebecca connected to the zipline and took off. Bailey walked to the makeshift fence that surrounded the platform and looked over. I walked beside her, resting my hand on the small of her back and looked down with her.

"That's a long fall," she said, turning to me.

"And that's a big gator," I pointed out. She whipped her head around and looked where I was pointing. A seven-and-a-half foot alligator laid on the side of the swamp. Flies buzzed around him, a turtle laying on his back. "Are you sure you want to do this?"

She turned back to me, her beautiful golden-brown eyes shimmering in the sun, and stared at me with unmatched excitement. "I want to go first."

I chuckled, nodding. Kelsey helped to strap her into the pulley and told her, "Whenever you're ready!" She lifted her feet off the platform and took off down the line. She screamed with a mixture of excitement and laughter, as she continued down.

As she got closer to the next platform I could hear Rebecca instruct her to brake. I could see her slow down as she got to the edge of the platform, swinging her feet to the edge and pulling herself onto the platform. Rebecca helped unstrap her, and I stepped up to take my turn.

I breathed deeply, staring down at Bailey. She still smiled. God she was beautiful. I lifted my feet as my descent began. I burst through the air, the wind pushing back on me. The feeling was like flying, so freeing. I glanced down at the scene below me, taking in the beauty of nature. I heard Rebecca tell me to brake and I moved my hand behind the pulley, slowing down and coming to a stop five feet from the platform.

Bailey giggled as I dangled in the air, waiting for Rebecca to reel me in. As my feet planted firmly on the platform, Bailey ran to me, wrapping her arms around me. She looked up at me, happiness glittering in her eyes. "Thank you so much for this," she sighed, laying her head on my chest.

After we went through all fifteen courses, varying in length and speed, we headed back to my apartment. When we got there, I opened the door, and we were hit in the face with the smell of tomatoes, garlic, and oregano. The spaghetti sauce I had on simmer since earlier that morning was almost done.

"What smells so good in here?" Bailey asked, walking in and taking in a big whiff of the air.

I smiled. "Homemade spaghetti sauce. I know how much you love spaghetti, so I figured I would pull out all the stops and make my special sauce for you."

She giggled. "Special sauce, huh?"

I could feel the red flooding my face as my eyes widened. "I didn't..."

"I know, Clay. I'm just giving you a hard time," she laughed, resting her head on my chest. I wrapped my arms around her, holding her as close to my body as I could. Being in her presence, feeling her touch, was enough to put my wild mind at ease. She calmed me, soothed me. She made me better.

I let go of her, taking her hand, and turning to the kitchen. "I want you to help me finish."

"I would love to!" She zoomed around me, pulling a pot out of the cabinet and filling it with water. "I'll start the noodles."

I smiled, watching her go through her motions. She started humming a happy tune, one that was vaguely familiar to me. I made my way to the pot simmering on the stove, the smells wafting out and flowing through the air, filling our noses with the delicious smell.

I grabbed a wooden spoon, dipping out some of the sauce and turned to Bailey. "Official taste test."

She turned around, opening her mouth wide. As she tasted the sauce, her eyes lit up. "Oh my god, Clay, that is so good. What did you put in it?"

"A little oregano and basil, a hint of nutmeg, two cloves of garlic. My secret ingredient is white wine. It just gives the sauce that extra pop," I winked. I bit my lip, staring into her eyes. All I could see in my reflection was happiness. For the first time in a very long time, I saw happiness in my reflection. And the reason for my happiness stared back at me.

I leaned in, my lips meeting hers as I savored her taste. The taste of the sauce still on her tongue as mine met hers. I lifted her up, placing her on the counter next to the sink. The kiss intensified, the kitchen heating up for reasons other than the bubbling sauce on the stove.

I wrapped my arm around her, sliding her closer to my body. I took her bottom lip in between my teeth, gently pulling on it as

I pulled my head back, smiling at her. "I could really get used to this."

"Used to what, Clay?" Bailey asked, quirking her eyebrow and cocking her head to the side.

"This. Me and you, cooking together in the kitchen, kissing. Enjoying being with each other. This is what love is, isn't it?"

"I think so," she sighed, resting her forehead against mine as we stared deep into one another's soul.

End Game

Things between Kenney and I had hit a snag. Something had been off with him for the last few months following New Years. He had been cold towards me, barely saying two words when we had seen each other. I had tried to strike up conversations with him. I would walk outside with him to smoke. All I ever received in return was 'Yeah', 'Uh huh', 'okay' followed by eye rolls and angry glares.

I was getting worried. Bailey and Kenney had a really strong relationship. While he wasn't her biological dad, he *was* her father at the end of the day. He had practically raised her. He spent more time with her than anyone else.

His opinion mattered to me because I knew it mattered to Bailey. I felt like if I lost Kenney, Bailey would soon follow. After all, she had known him almost all her life, and me only a few months. I knew in my mind she would take his side if things went bad.

A knock came at my door around noon, waking me up from a deep sleep. I blinked my eyes a couple of times while my brain booted up from sleep mode. Another knock forced me out of bed.

I opened the door, rubbing my eyes with the back of my hand. To my surprise, Bailey stood before me, soaked from the rain. Her gray shirt stuck to her body, her hair tied into tiny strings, makeup running down her face like she was melting.

She stepped past me, putting her head down. I closed the door, slowly turning around. My mind was racing, something wasn't right. I knew she had come down from school for the weekend, but I thought she was spending it with her parents. "What's wrong, Bailey?"

She looked at me, biting her bottom lip as she contemplated what to say. She bounced from leg to leg, her hands steadily shaking. "Daddy…" she started before a tear slipped from her eye, tracing her already wet and smeared makeup all the way down.

"Bailey, talk to me," I pleaded, my expression falling at the same rate as my heart. I felt the pounding sensation in my chest, the growing black pit consuming me.

She inhaled, taking a deep breath to calm herself down. "We got into a fight," she said before closing her eyes. She chewed on the bottom of her lip, trying to gain her composure and not breakdown.

"What do you mean by a fight?" I already knew it was about me. I just knew it had to be.

"He thinks I'm spending too much time with you. He says I'm not focusing on my coursework or soccer because of you. I tried to tell him you were helping me with school and told him how well I was doing in my classes. My grades are so good, I made the Dean's List! He just wouldn't listen. He got so mad."

I wrapped my arms around her, pulling her into me. I sat there, just holding her, comforting her. I didn't know what to say or do. I was the root of the problem, how do I fix that? She pushed her forehead into my chest as tears and her wet hair began to dampen my shirt. She sobbed, taking in deep breaths and exhaling slowly as she let out her emotions. Tiny breaths escaped in between sobs and deep breaths, almost pushing her to hyperventilate.

"I'm right here, Bailey," I whispered into her hair as I slowly rubbed her back. Just a light touch, running up and down the middle of her back, trying to ease her pain. "Shhhh."

As her sobs started to slow, her breathing returned to normal, and she glanced up at me. "I didn't know where else to go, Clay. I'm sorry for just showing up out of the blue."

"Bailey, you never have to apologize to me for showing up. I am always here for you. My door is always open to you. I just wish I could do more to help you."

"You're here, Clay. Being around you, being in your arms and embracing your warmth, that's what I needed. What I still need."

I leaned back, smiling at her. "Why don't you go get dried off and changed? You can wear a pair of my shorts and one of my shirts. Then we can just lay in bed."

She nodded, blinking her eyes a few times to keep the few tears that were left at bay. I let go and went to grab a change of clothes for her as she made her way to the bathroom to dry off.

I just couldn't understand why Kenney would be so mad about her spending time with me. Why did it even get to the point of an argument? I just couldn't wrap my head around it, and honestly it pissed me off.

I grabbed a pair of basketball shorts and a plain white t-shirt and brought it to the bathroom. I knocked gently on the closed door. "I'm decent," she half-heartedly chuckled from inside the bathroom.

I cracked the door open, peeking around it. Bailey stood at the sink, the towel spread across it, her hands planted on top of the counter. She stared into her reflection, never turning to meet my eye.

"Are you okay?" I asked, setting the clothes down beside her hands. I moved my hand to her back, caressing it again as I walked closer to her.

"Everything was going perfect between us, and now this. It isn't fair that he's acting like this. I'm nineteen now! I don't have to deal with his shit. I shouldn't have to deal with him acting like this." She started shaking as her hands faded from red to white, her nose twitching as she stared herself down in the mirror.

I wanted nothing more than to take away this anger and hurt she felt and make it all better. But I couldn't, and I felt awful. I moved behind her, wrapping my arms around her waist and nuzzling my face into her neck. I pressed tiny kisses along the side of her neck, holding her closely.

We laid in bed later that evening, the sound of the rain beating against the window drowning out the silence. We had been laying there for hours, holding each other, staring into each other's soul. It was comforting just to be there with her. Just to feel her touch. Just to look into her eyes.

The rain had poured nonstop all day. From the time I'd woken up that afternoon to now. Flood warnings flashed across our phones, and the parking lot of my apartment was flooded with no way in or out. "Please stay tonight," I pleaded with her. "It's way too dangerous to drive in this."

She sighed as she looked at me. "He's not going to be happy if I do that. I need to head home."

"Bailey, look outside. There is literally no way you're driving out of this parking lot. The water is over halfway up the tires."

Her eyes fluttered from side to side as she stared at me. "You're right, Clay, but how am I supposed to tell him that? He'll flip out again."

"Tell your mom. She knows him best. She'll be able to calm him down if he gets upset. She has to understand that you can't drive in this." I hoped anyway.

She nodded slowly, pulling her phone out from underneath her stomach where it had been situated since we'd laid down. She sent her mom a message and set the phone back down, slowly looking back up at me. "Well, now we wait."

"No waiting. We continue our night. Enjoy each other and not let anything else bother us. You've told your mom. Now you can relax," I said, brushing her hair behind her ear. I placed my index finger under her chin and lifting her head up. "I love you, Bailey."

She opened her mouth to speak but was interrupted by the buzzing of her phone. She glanced down at the phone as 'Daddy' flashed across the screen. My heart dropped into my stomach, and judging from the look on her face so did Bailey's. "What do I do?" she asked.

I hesitated, not knowing. He was her dad, despite how he was acting. "You should answer it. If he is mad, ignoring his call will just infuriate him even more. Maybe he hasn't even talked to your mom and he's calling to apologize." Did I believe the second option? Absolutely not, but stranger things have happened.

She took a deep breath before answering the phone. When she did, she put it on speakerphone and laid it down in between us. "Hello?""I know damn well you don't think you're staying over there tonight. You need to get home, now." I could hear the anger in his voice, like the sound of fire roaring out of control.

"Daddy," Bailey started.

"Don't 'daddy' me. This isn't up for discussion. You're coming home, and you're coming home now."

"I can't get out of the parking lot of Clay's apartment complex. It's flooded and the roads between here and home are flooded, too." She was doing everything she could to counter his anger, to help him see her side of the situation.

"Should have thought about that before you left the house in a tizzy. Get in the car, and drive home. Now." The floodgates opened as Bailey let her tears fall. They streaked down her face, reminiscent of the way the rain was running down the windows. Her soft and quiet sobs began, and I couldn't take it anymore.

There was no way I was letting Bailey put herself in a dangerous situation like that.

I picked up the phone and rolled out of bed. I walked out of the room, trying to distance him from her. "Kenney…"

"I don't want to fucking talk to you. Put Bailey back on the phone." The anger in his voice pouring out caused my skin to crawl.

I gritted my teeth, trying to keep my cool through the situation. "Look, I can't, in good conscience, let Bailey drive in this. It has been pouring all day. The roads are flooded, and she can't get out of the parking lot."

"I don't give a fuck." He was practically spitting through the phone. "I want her home, away from you, now."

"What did I do to piss you off so much? We were fine a few weeks ago. Now you've flipped the script on me for no reason." I heard the frustration in my voice mounting; the urge to yell making its way up my throat, threatening to erupt.

"You're a prick who thinks you're better than everyone. You think you can just waltz in here and take Bailey away from us. You think you're the greatest thing to happen to her. Guess what, you aren't."

"What are you even talking about Kenney? I don't think I'm better than anyone, I'm not trying to take her away from you. I encourage her to spend time with y'all just as much as she spends time with me." And it was the truth. I placed great importance on family, and I never wanted to steal Bailey away from them. I wanted to become part of the family, not tear it apart.

"Listen, mother fucker, I don't like you. I don't want anything to do with you anymore. In fact, I want you out of my life. The sooner the better."

"I'm not going anywhere." It was time for me to take a stand. I loved Bailey, and I would fight for her. I wasn't going to continue to be disrespected by him. "I don't care if you like me. It's Bailey that I'm dating, not you. She isn't going anywhere tonight. You may be willing to put her in danger, but I'm not and I won't."

I hung up the phone, letting my arm slowly fall down my side as I stared into nothingness. What had I done to deserve this? Was Bailey willing to stand by my side? Was this going to be the end of us?

"Clay," I heard Bailey quietly call from behind me. I squeezed my eyes shut before turning around. She was standing behind me in the doorway of my room. She had heard every word.

"I'm... I'm sorry Bailey. I just couldn't let him keep talking to you like that."

She ran to me, wrapping her arms around my neck. I held her, listening to her whimpers in between sobs. It broke my heart to see her like this. I kissed the top of her head, closing my eyes to hold back my own tears.

"I'll understand if you can't be with me anymore," I said, letting the tears fall into her hair. "Family is the most important thing, and I don't want to come in between that. I don't want to be the reason you two are fighting."

She looked up at me, the tears no longer streaming from her eyes. A look of seriousness had replaced her somber expression. "I'm not going anywhere, Clay. I told you, I will always fight for you. I love you more than I have ever loved another man before, and I'm not willing to just throw everything away. I'll fight for you, I won't let this come in between us. Forever."

I was at a loss for words. I didn't expect her to fight for me like this. Nobody had ever fought for me like this. In the past, when push had come to shove, it was easier for them to leave than to fight for me. Bailey was different. This was different.

"Always."

To Be Continued in Sunflower Kisses Book 2

T hanks for joining Clay and Bailey in their journey as a new, young couple!

Did you enjoy *The Seeds of Love: Sunflower Kisses Book 1?* Are you excited for Book 2? Here's what you can do next!

If you loved the book and have a moment to spare, it would mean a lot to me if you would leave a short review. Your help in spreading the word about my work is much appreciated.

The next book in the *Sunflower Kisses* series will be available in the coming months. Get your FREE download of *(Not) Alone,* the gripping story that delves into the realities of struggling with mental health, plus be notified on the progress of *Sunflower Kisses*

Book 2 as well as mental health tips, giveaways, and pre-release specials at:

T.B. Wittkofsky is a storyteller, educator, and community builder who uses his personal experiences to help others rise with their stories. With a background in marketing, communications, and mental health advocacy, his work blends strategy with heart. T.B. has taught courses on branding, social media, and entrepreneurship, guiding students and creatives through the evolving digital landscape.

After overcoming challenges like addiction, job loss, and financial instability, T.B. embraced a life on the road in an RV with his wife and three dogs, finding clarity, healing, and inspiration in the journey. He now leads Adventure with Coffee, a blog and podcast that celebrates connection through culture, travel, and, of course, coffee.

As the former president of the North Brunswick Chamber of Commerce and founder of Tea With Coffee Media, T.B. has helped countless entrepreneurs and small businesses find their voice. His advocacy work, including panels on mental health and representation in fiction, underscores his mission to create safe, inclusive spaces for honest storytelling.

Whether mentoring writers, consulting on marketing campaigns, or writing stories that reflect lived truths, T.B. shows up with compassion, curiosity, and an unwavering belief in the power of the narrative.

www.ingramcontent.com/pod-product-compliance
Lightning Source LLC
Chambersburg PA
CBHW050849190726

48286CB00007B/2302